Fire Under Snow

Fire Under Snow

DOROTHY VERNON

G.K. Hall & Co. • Chivers Press
Waterville, Maine USA   Bath, England

This Large Print edition is published by G.K. Hall & Co., USA
and by Chivers Press, England.

Published in 2001 in the U.S. by arrangement with
Juliet Burton Literary Agency.

Published in 2001 in the U.K. by arrangement with the author.

U.S. Hardcover 0-7838-9542-9 (Paperback Series Edition)
U.K. Hardcover 0-7540-4733-4 (Chivers Large Print)

The text of this Large Print edition is unabridged.
Other aspects of the book may vary from the original edition.

Set in 16 pt. Plantin by Minnie B. Raven.

Printed in the United States on permanent paper.

British Library Cataloguing-in-Publication Data available

Library of Congress Cataloging-in-Publication Data

Vernon, Dorothy.
    Fire under snow / Dorothy Vernon.
        p. cm.
    ISBN 0-7838-9542-9 (lg. print : sc : alk. paper)
    1. Fires — Casualties — Fiction.   2. Large type books.   I.
Title.
PR6072.E737 F57 2001
823'.914—dc21   2001026375

Fire Under Snow

Chapter One

It all reopened so very quietly. When Lorraine's friend Jessica asked her if she'd care to join a party of girls on a night out the following Thursday, she was delighted to accept. Thursday was her birthday, although neither Jessica nor any of the other girls in the office where they both worked knew this. Not wanting any fuss, she decided to keep the knowledge to herself, but she would secretly look on the outing as a birthday celebration.

Lorraine's appearance gave the impression of amazing self-confidence. It was an illusion, the opposite being more in keeping with the truth. The dainty perfection of her features and the allure of her slender yet shapely body failed to give her confidence. It had not always been so. Once she had been proud-walking, swinging through life with her chin high and fully aware of her exceptional beauty.

Three years ago she had been involved in something that had caused her much distress; something she still couldn't think about rationally, which had temporarily robbed her of her looks and seemed to have stolen her confidence for all time. It was odd, because she could look in a mirror and see that the scars that had marred her face were gone. Her hands were smooth and supple, no longer mutilated. Yet she couldn't accept it. She still felt scarred and ugly. Perhaps subconsciously she didn't want to accept it because handsome looks had become linked in her mind with a less handsome character. Jamie had had the face of an angel. To her deep grief she had found it to be a façade concealing a callous and indifferent nature. Jamie had proved himself to be a weakling and a coward. How was she to know, when she accepted Jessica's invitation, that she was re-opening that black chapter in her life?

Even when Jessica named The Black Cat, a nightclub famed for attracting big-name artists, as their destination, no shadow fell to dull her happiness. Certainly no involuntary shiver of apprehension touched her as she mentally reviewed her wardrobe and decided the occasion called for an evening gown, a frivolity she'd had no cause to indulge in for a long time.

Jessica, who adored spending money irrespective of whether it was her own or someone else's, insisted on accompanying her on her spending spree. Again she was happy to have her friend's company, thinking she would offer gentle guidance and practical assistance. She had failed to take into account, however, Jessica's overwhelming personality. Later, on Thursday evening itself, when she zipped herself into the cling-fit jersey dress, she thought she must have been crazy to allow herself to be

8

talked into buying it. She hadn't taken much interest in her appearance at the time, allowing Jessica and the equally enthusiastic sales assistant to be her mirror. The dress, virginal white and classically simple, had appealed to her because of its unassuming quality when it was displayed on its dress hanger. Her body molded it into a different proposition altogether. It was a show-off dress, a dress that compelled the eye and refused to slink into obscurity, the kind of dress she would have worn with panache in the old days.

The club was packed to suffocating capacity. She couldn't even claim to be cold and had to relinquish her coat to the cloakroom attendant, along with the coats and wraps of her friends. Her eye caught the larger-than-life-size portrait of the star of the show. Her consternation about the dress was suddenly forgotten in the face of this new torment of infinitely greater magnitude. In any case, the dress didn't look all that conspicuous in these surroundings. Amid so many slinkily and skimpily clad females, it was neither outrageous nor all that eye-catching.

As they went in search of their table, Jessica touched her arm and asked in kindly concern, "Are you all right, Lorraine? You look as if you've seen a ghost."

She hadn't seen him yet, the ghost from her past. Catching sight of his picture like that had been sufficient to blanch her features.

"I didn't know that Jamie Gray was topping the bill."

"Really? How odd." Odd that she didn't know? Odd that it should have this effect on her? She must be careful. "The office has been buzzing with it and it's been in all the newspapers. We were tremendously lucky to get tickets at such short notice. A cancellation, I believe."

"I've got all his records," one of the girls said dreamily.

"I'm so excited," another said, "I don't know how I'm going to wait until he comes on. He doesn't make his appearance until the end of the second half of the show. They say he comes down among the audience and some girls even get to kiss him. I'll die if he picks me."

"You're too young to die," Jessica said dryly, "so it's probably just as well our table is so far back. He'll never get past the she-wolves in the first three rows."

Lorraine let out a slow sigh of relief. A less pleased member of the party, Claire, said querulously, "Why couldn't we have got a table at the front?"

"Because we didn't decide soon enough, silly. We only found out about" — Jessica's eyes rested mischievously on Lorraine — "you know," she said mysteriously, although Lorraine realized by the looks the others exchanged that she was the only one mystified.

She sank lower in her seat. Surely they couldn't have found out about that? She had changed her job and kept her past strictly to herself.

At the time, Aunt Leonora had wanted her to make her home with her in Kittiwake Bay, but she had resisted the temptation to go to the cottage for some "home spoiling," knowing it was best for her to cling to her independence. She had been hurt, yes. But she would survive. She had to. In a way she had been glad that her father hadn't lived to witness the tragedy. And yet, as her mother had predeceased her father by several years, it had thrown an unfair burden on Aunt Leonora, her mother's sister, who was young enough in outlook to be her contemporary and who had been her mainstay, her devoted companion and friend.

She would never have got through those dark days without her. She had a lot to be grateful to her for. Never once had she said, "I told you so," although it must have crossed her mind that, had Lorraine listened to her counsel, the tragedy wouldn't have happened. Aunt Leonora had seen through Jamie from the first, and she had advised her to tread with caution. But twenty, as she had been then, isn't noted for being a cautious age. Her youth, coupled with an impulsive and headstrong nature, made it inevitable that she follow the dictates of her heart and suffer the consequences.

It did not help that her heart had played her false. It had not been as totally committed as it had led her to believe. It had healed before her pride. It had been a bitter healing, a destroying healing, taking her sweet and trusting nature and leaving her with an unattractive wariness that was often taken for aloofness. She found it difficult to respond to kindly overtures and didn't blame people for not bothering with her. She was deeply indebted to Jessica for persevering with her friendship.

Jessica was a beautifully uncomplicated, forthright type of girl. The same age as Lorraine — twenty-three — she had taken her under her wing, indoctrinating her in office matters, helping her to find a small, reasonably priced apartment.

When she first met Jessica the scars had been very much in evidence. Meeting new people at that time was always an ordeal. They reacted in one or more of the following ways: with horror, with embarrassment or with feigned indifference. Not so Jessica. "What happened? Were you in a car crash, fire, or what?" No revulsion, no embarrassment, just kindly interest.

"A fire."

"I take it you don't want to talk about it?"

"Not anymore. I don't want to rake over the dead ash. I want to forget."

"He must have been a rat."

"Who must?"

"You're telling me there isn't more to it than you're giving out? If I poked around in the ashes, it's a certainty I'd find some guy at the heart of the matter."

"I evicted him from my heart some time ago."

"If you say so," her friend had replied, a disbelieving look on her face.

She came back to the present to hear Jessica say, "I like to get here early. You can see who's coming in. Don't look around" — giving the cue for a swivel of heads because not one of them, including Lorraine, could resist the provocative temptation of sneaking a look — "but here comes Noel Britton."

"Who is Noel Britton?" Lorraine asked.

"The owner of this nightclub and also the head of the N. J. Britton Recording Company. He operates under the Best of Britton label and he's got Jamie Gray, plus the cream of the recording artists, under contract."

"Impressive," Lorraine conceded.

"His achievements? Or the man himself?" Jessica challenged. "And the only Mrs. Britton is his mother."

He was tall, standing head and shoulders above most men, with a lean, loose-limbed virility that would dress well in casual jeans but could never look more impressive than now in immaculate evening clothes. His thick black hair had a blue sheen under the wreathing cigar and cigarette smoke. His features were strong — hard was the word that flung itself into her mind — the deeply suntanned skin tight over the angular bones, the hint of sensuality about the mouth providing no saving grace as it added to the impression of strength rather than detracting from it.

He was smoking a cigar. He drew it from his lips and a perfect ring formed above his head. It took just the time his steel-gray eyes rested on her for Lorraine to know that the smoke halo was not symbolic of sainthood. His glance, without warmth and filled with contempt at being stared at by a party of girls, was more searing than the flames that had scarred her flesh three years ago. How could a passing stranger have this effect on her? How could she feel so scorched?

Now that his patronizing eyes were turned from her, her own unashamedly followed his descent down a series of steps — the back tables were set on raised levels to provide a better view of the stage — until he reached his off-center, front table.

The resident band took over from the canned music that had been blaring from the loud-speakers. The compère's opening gags were corny, predictable and definitely risqué, yet were delivered in a pleasing style that obviously made him a well-liked figure at The Black Cat. Or "The Mucky Moggy," as he, Shane Peters, called it.

He wisecracked for several minutes, warming up the crowd, and then vacated the stage as the Kittens, The Black Cat's tall, leggy dancing troupe, bounded on stage to wolf whistles as

14

skirts flounced up to show a frilly garter or a peep of white thigh above a black stocking top. A female vocalist came on next, then a comedian, followed by the return of Shane Peters to introduce the audience participation spot.

Anyone who had a birthday, retirement, wedding anniversary and so forth to celebrate, and whose name had been previously handed in to reception, was invited to go up on the stage for a chat and to receive a bouquet of flowers or a bottle of champagne. As the spotlight centered on those called up, Lorraine was pleased she hadn't mentioned that it was her birthday to Jessica. It was just the sort of thing Jessica reveled in, and she would have been hard pressed to resist the temptation of giving in her name.

The spotlight ran across the room to pinpoint a pretty dark-haired girl who was on a night out to celebrate her forthcoming marriage. She stood up and waved before going up on the stage. Next came a newly engaged couple who went up holding hands, happy smiles on their faces. A camera clicked to record their proud moment. A silver anniversary pair followed them, also sweetly holding hands.

"And now we have a birthday girl," Shane Peters announced. "A young lady by the name of Lorraine. Where are you, Lorraine?"

Lorraine — no surname. Even as she stiffened, she told herself she was being silly. Someone else who was called Lorraine was also celebrating her birthday. Even so, she held her breath as she waited for him to call out the table number so that the spotlight could pick out the birthday girl.

The table number was the one she was sitting at. Her worst fears founded, her eyes flashed to Jessica, whose smug smile proclaimed her the culprit. How could she do this to her? How had she found out? The spotlight swooped and drenched her in its beam.

"I think our birthday girl is shy. How about a round of applause to encourage the little lady?" Shane Peters said, putting his own hands together.

The other participants had all been good sports; every one of them had cheerfully entered into the spirit of the thing. There was no way she could gracefully duck out of this ordeal. "I'll talk to you later," she said to Jessica in a muttered aside as she rose to her feet.

The spotlight marked her progress down the steps. She held her chin high and kept her eyes front until she reached the stage. It was raised, obviously mounted by steps. Everyone else had seemed to know automatically the point to make for. In her acute self-consciousness she was less perceptive and faltered.

"To your left, Lorraine," Shane Peters instructed.

Even as her brain worked out which way was left, a hand like an electric charge cupped her elbow, guiding her the right way. She looked up to thank the man who had jumped to her rescue, and the words dried in her mouth. Yet why was she surprised to see it was Noel Britton? Hadn't the instinctive reaction of her skin to his touch identified him as the disturbing stranger?

"Thank you," she managed.

He nodded curtly in acknowledgment, but his steel-gray eyes were kindly and not contemptuous. His hand left her elbow, leaving her feeling strangely deserted and alone even though Shane Peters's hand was reaching down to assist her the rest of the way.

"Don't be nervous. Shane will look after you."

From a distance, by his style of dress and the way he did his hair, the show's compère could be mistaken for a much younger man. Close up, it was a shock to realize that his age couldn't be much short of fifty.

"That's a lovely dress you're wearing. Isn't she a little firecracker, folks? I understand it's your birthday today. How old are you, darling?"

"Twenty-three." He was holding the microphone too far away, and it came out as a whisper.

"Speak up, darling. I can't hear you."

"Twenty-three." This time he brought the microphone up close and she appeared to be shouting.

"That's a lovely age to be. I wish I were twenty-three. Still" — his eyes danced with mischief — "I can wait."

He gave the cue to the stagehand to come on

with a bouquet of flowers, which he took from the youth and handed to Lorraine. "Happy birthday, darling. Do I get a little kiss?" he inquired impishly.

She knew she was being maneuvered for laughs, but she wasn't quick enough to do anything about it. He had deliberately put the flowers in her hands at an awkward angle. He leaned forward to kiss her and stopped. "This could be dangerous," he said, carefully pointing the stalks the other way. The audience loved it. They rocked in their seats with laughter. Shane Peters bent to kiss her and squeezed her hand in token apology as if to say, "It's only a bit of fun." Then she was allowed to leave the stage.

A hand came up to assist her down the steps. The tingle in her fingertips told her it belonged to Noel Britton.

Once again she thanked him for his kindness.

He said, "Would I be right in thinking you feel too much in the public eye as it is and that it would prolong the agony if I invited you to my table for a drink?"

"Yes, you would be right."

"Later, perhaps?" he said, his left eyebrow flaring in speculation.

"I think not. Thank you all the same, Mr. Britton."

"You have the advantage of me." Her green-flecked eyes challenged that. No one would ever have an advantage over Noel Britton. "I know you are called Lorraine, but I don't know your full name."

Smiling coolly, she said, "That's all right. I do."

He wasn't used to women withholding things from him. Their names . . . their bodies. The hand that had provided welcome assistance down the steps now was unwelcomely tight around her arm, a steel trap that would not free her until she gave him what he wanted.

There was no other way. She could have stood up against his greater physical strength and his iron will, but, as if the odds weren't already weighted in his favor, he had on his side the enthralled attention of every eye in the club, or so it seemed to Lorraine as she squirmed in embarrassment.

She surrendered her name with a dignified lift of her pointed little chin. "Lorraine Marshall." It secured her release. As she walked away from the tall, distinguished-looking figure, it was not all the other eyes she was most conscious of, but his eyes. Gray eyes that had regarded her with undisguised interest. Were they following her now to derive the last scrap of amusement? The cruel clamp on her arm had provided the clue. He was the type who would delight in this kind of taunting.

She resumed her seat, hoping her friends would refrain from commenting on her heightened color.

Jessica was looking at her in awe, admiration and envy. "You move in high circles," she gasped. "What did he say to you?"

"Surely you heard every word he said, and also my replies once he'd stopped fooling around with the mike."

"Not the compère — Noel Britton."

"Nothing much," she said, dismissing him with a shrug. "What on earth made you do that to me? You know how much I hate to be the center of attention. How did you know it was my birthday?"

"Ah — that would be telling."

Lorraine supplied the answer herself. "You got it from Records. It was a mean trick."

"I'm sorry," Jessica said, not looking sorry at all. "Me, now, I would have lapped it up. Honestly, I didn't realize you would find it so awful. Anyway, you can relax now. It's over."

She hoped it was. But it was a small sliver of hope. One that, nevertheless, grew stronger until she could rest easy, having convinced herself that Jamie wouldn't have witnessed her impromptu stage appearance from behind the scenes. He had come a long way in three years. He was very much the big star now. In the event of his having arrived at the club, he would be safely tucked away in his dressing room, either putting on his stage clothes or relaxing. He wouldn't be standing in the wings, gleaning all he could from the other acts as he had done in the struggling days of his career when she knew him.

He had been like an unpolished diamond

then. The potential was there — he had the voice and the melting, little-boy looks — but he'd lacked the sparkle. That had somehow been acquired along the way. He'd always talked big. He had promised himself a large house in the country with its own heated swimming pool, a car with his personalized number plate, a holiday home abroad. It wasn't the dangling carrot of a life of luxury that had attracted her to him. If anything, that would have put her off, because she wasn't grasping by nature. She would have given anyone who suggested otherwise the sharp edge of her tongue. Easygoing for the most part, she could speak her mind when the occasion demanded it. Her father used to say, "You've inherited your mother's fine features, high cheekbones, heart-shaped face, beautiful green-flecked eyes and golden flood of hair, but, heaven help you, girl, my temper!"

So it wasn't the things Jamie promised; it was Jamie himself. His winsome appeal had spoken to her strongly, and she had mistaken her responses for love. In a way it might have been love. There are different levels of loving. She had loved him with her eyes and not her heart. He was twenty-five then, although he'd looked about seventeen. In the full magnificence of male youth, he was like a god on a pedestal to her. At first glance there had seemed about him an innocence and purity that was almost feminine. Later she realized his gentleness was a form of weakness, not a praiseworthy characteristic in anyone, but worse in a man than in a woman. There was no saving sweetness anywhere in his nature. The softly rounded curve of cheek and chin and the fullness of his mouth masked a hard streak of indifference that was to bring her more pain than if he'd lifted his hand to her in cruelty and assaulted her. Success was more than a dream he would work hard to realize; it was an obsession. If anyone got in his way, that was just too bad — for them.

She had reasoned all this out later. At the time her brain hadn't been functioning too well. She had still been mourning the death of her father, so perhaps all the tears weren't for herself. The thought had even crossed her mind that the tears were some kind of delayed reaction, a penance she had to pay for not being able to weep for her father. The death of her father had shocked her so profoundly that she had been too numb to feel, to shed the normal tears of grief. It was as though Jamie's defection pulled her round and unlocked the tears she hadn't been able to shed a few bitter months before when her father had died. She was made to feel, cry, sorrow, and, painful as it was, it proved her salvation.

If she'd known that Jamie was topping the bill she would have made some excuse to decline Jessica's invitation to join the party. Now, despite everything, a tiny part of her was glad she had accepted in ignorance. She was curious to know how the intervening years had dealt with Jamie. Three years isn't all that long when measured against time; but, measured against events, it can sometimes seem to be a lifetime. They had been good years for Jamie. He'd risen from an unknown supporting artist to a top recording star. Had he been able to adapt? Was he equal to it? Suddenly acquired wealth brings its own crop of casualties. Pressures build up, false props are relied on. The Jamie she had known was not noted for his sagacity. He was neither prudent nor levelheaded, and she knew from bitter experience that he crumbled in a crisis.

Her own foolishness struck her. It was incredible that she could still worry about him after all that had passed between them. In any case, it was totally unnecessary. He had his own built-in buoyancy, so that, whoever else sank, he would always remain afloat. He was a superficial person but a likable one; if all else failed, he could charm his way out of the darkest corner. He had even made it seem right when he . . .

No more time for thoughts. They were playing Jamie's music now. Shane Peters made the announcement, the velvet curtains swung away and the spotlight centered on Jamie's dipped, golden head. He wore a white satin suit and a deeply frilled midnight-blue shirt that was casually unbuttoned to reveal a medallion suspended on a chunky gold chain. In the old days the chain would have been silver. Apart from that, he was just as she remembered him. He had more polish, more confidence, but, even though he was three years older, which brought his age up to twenty-eight, he still looked seventeen.

How do you do it, Jamie? she wondered, just as she was to wonder how such a lightweight person, whose keynote was insincerity, could reach out to an audience and within minutes hold that audience in the palm of his hand.

He began by lifting his chin slowly for maximum dramatic effect. His candyfloss smile — sweet but with no substance to it — singled out every female in the room, making her feel as though he was lighting up just for her. His program was more varied than in the old days. He switched from a new hit to a nostalgic oldie; one minute her foot was tapping, the next her throat was constricting. So much she remembered; so much more she'd forgotten. He put down his guitar and went into an informal chat session. Although it was new, she remembered it was something he'd wanted to introduce. But the hesitation, the break in his voice, the little laugh — these things were familiar. They were tricks he'd applied in the old days when a note was beyond his pitch. He used to spend hours before his mirror getting the timing right, perfecting his facial expressions to make it seem off-the-cuff, ensuring that it had the ring of spontaneity.

When the curtain finally closed after three

encores — the audience would have kept him there all night — Jessica said breathlessly, "He's magic! What charisma!"

During his chat spot Jamie had announced that he would shortly be leaving for Las Vegas, where he was booked to appear. He'd also mentioned that he would be in the foyer after the show to sign copies of his latest record.

The girls were discussing this now. Jessica said, "I love him to bits. I'm going to buy a record and get him to autograph it."

Lorraine was the only one not eager to do the same. "I won't wait with you. I'll make my own way home."

"How?" one of the others said.

"I'll phone for a taxi."

"It will cost you the earth. Why don't you wait with us? Even if you don't want to buy a record, you're surely not going to miss the chance of seeing him up close."

Jessica was eyeing Lorraine shrewdly. She informed the girl who had just spoken, "Save your breath. Wild horses wouldn't drag Lorraine away. Talking of horses, you're a dark one, Lorraine." A tormenting yet not unkind smile touched her mouth. "I know why you don't want to meet Jamie Gray."

"You do?" Lorraine queried throatily.

"Correct me if I'm wrong," Jessica said with irritating slowness, "but I think you've got bigger fish to fry."

"Bigger fish?" Lorraine repeated stupidly.

"Don't play the innocent. We saw you and Noel Britton with your heads together. You were arranging to meet later. In fact, it's my belief that he's waiting for you right now at the bar. Do you deny it?"

Lorraine said, on a brittle laugh, "It seems I've been found out." Her brain was working frantically. If she didn't string along with this supposition of Jessica's, her kindhearted friend would never allow her to call a taxi and go home by herself. But she simply could not countenance the consequences of a face-to-face meeting with Jamie in these surroundings, under the eyes of her friends. Distasteful as it was to her to lie, she could see no other course.

"On your feet, then," Jessica urged briskly. "Don't keep the man waiting."

"What's the hurry? I'll wait until you go. It will be more seemly for him to join me then," she replied inventively.

"Sorry, but we're not going yet," Jessica said stoutly. "I've been through this before. Jamie Gray won't make his appearance until there's a healthy crowd in the foyer. In fact, we've time for another drink."

Which, in turn, would give Noel Britton ample time to finish his drink and remove himself from the bar, and then her lie would be uncovered. A furtive glance told her that he had already finished too much of his drink for her liking.

She contemplated the follow-up of being

found out. The girls might not think she'd told a lie. They might assume that Noel Britton had forgotten about her, in which case she would come in for a spot of good-natured teasing, which she wouldn't mind; but then, like the good sorts they were, they'd rally round and insist on her accompanying them to the foyer to meet Jamie. No!

She was on her feet in an instant. But even as she walked toward the bar she thought, *I must be out of my mind.* How could she carry this off? "I'll have that drink now, if it's all the same with you, Mr. Britton." No. Too coy. The odds were that he would have forgotten her. *Oh, please, let him look up and recognize me as the petrified girl whose assistance he came to earlier; make him remember inviting me to his table for a drink afterward.*

Her plea was not answered. No heavenly power was going to offer a helping hand, and it did not seem likely that she could look for earthly intervention, either. She was going to have to do this all by herself.

She was almost level with him now and still his eyes were directed away from her. A frown transformed his mouth to stone. His severe profile was not confidence-inspiring. It was an interesting face, but carved in this effigy of thought, bereft of the Galahad smile he'd given her earlier as he guided her to the steps leading to the stage and stripped of the amusement that had later brushed his features, it was an austere and forbidding face.

"Mr. Britton?" Oh, dear, surely she could do better than that scared whisper. "Mr. Britton?"

This time his chin lifted in response and his eyes fixed on her in cool regard. If there was no recognition, there was, mercifully, no blankness, either.

The back of her neck was burning with the knowledge that she was being closely watched by the rest of her party. She wasn't going to get down on her knees and beg for his attention.

The length and aggressiveness of her return gaze caused the faintest raising of his eyebrows. "Miss Marshall, I believe?" A smile that was closely related to a sneer curved his mouth. "I take it you've changed your mind about having that drink with me," he said without surprise, as if he'd known all along that she would reconsider.

It would pain her to say yes. Any drink offered with such overbearing conceit would choke her. Yet the alternative of stalking off on an abrupt refusal and having to rejoin her friends was even more unpalatable.

She smiled, content to know that the girls would see only the smile and that its lack of sweetness could not be detected at this distance. "How can I possibly say no to such gallant enthusiasm. I'll have —" A mischievous look came to her eyes. "Now, let me see; what drink would most suitably fit the occasion? I know! A bitter lemon, please."

A look of grudging respect flitted over his

face as he grappled to understand her strange behavior. Girls who made the approach didn't normally use frost tactics. "Can we start again?" he said, sending her a smile that was on its way to being conciliatory. "It would give me enormous pleasure if you'd have that drink with me now, Miss Marshall."

"Thank you, Mr. Britton. I'm delighted to accept. May I still have a bitter lemon, please, simply because I haven't got the head for stronger stuff and I like its tangy taste?"

He signaled the barman, and the drinks — her bitter lemon and his more potent choice — were placed before them promptly.

"Did you enjoy the show?" he inquired.

"Every minute of it. Well — almost," she amended, in oblique reference to the part she'd been made to play in the audience participation spot, which she hadn't liked at all.

The look of intelligence that came to his eyes told her that he was on her wavelength. "And Jamie Gray? What do you think of him?"

"He's a very talented young man," she replied guardedly.

Her lack of enthusiasm was noted without comment. "Would you like to meet him?"

"Not particularly."

"That's a great pity. At closing time, to send him off to the States in good spirits, a party is being held for him here at the club. I was thinking of asking you to come as my guest." A deliberate pause. "What about it?"

How cruel fate could be. He was the most exciting man she had ever met and she wished she could accept. Her reasons for avoiding Jamie earlier on still applied, and were even more pressing. If she couldn't bring herself to meet Jamie again after all this time under the kindly eyes of her friends, she certainly could not voluntarily let Noel Britton witness the event.

It irked her to admit it, but, from the moment he was pointed out to her, she had been too aware of him. From a distance his presence had agitated her pulse beat; his nearness had an even more disturbing effect. It jangled her pulse into a frenzy. It was an assault on her senses and not at all to her liking. She preferred to walk at a slow pace into friendship these days, having learned her lesson with Jamie. Take time to know a person, come to terms with their pet foibles and those small, human peculiarities. Her instincts of self-preservation — the ones her letdown over Jamie had made acute — rebelled at being tipped into the turbulent depths of a relationship, which was what she felt was happening then.

So perhaps it was just as well she had to say, "Sorry, no."

"I gather you're not a Jamie Gray fan. There will be other personalities there — and *me*," he said with emphasis, as if that were an irresistible temptation. As, indeed, it almost was. "Care to change your mind?"

"I — can't."

"Can't?" Irritation crossed his face, indicating that *can't* was a word he refused to acknowledge.

She hadn't deliberately set out to thwart him. She thought about explaining that she couldn't attend the party with him because of her involvement with Jamie. If it had been a sealed and finished chapter in her far-distant past, she would undoubtedly have said something. But it was too painfully close and still tied her. It clung, like ivy to a tree, its poisonous tendrils choking her freedom. She had been a coward, turning her back on something unpleasant. How much wiser it would have been to contact Jamie . . . see him and talk to him so that she would know in her mind that it was over between them. Perhaps there would be time to arrange a meeting before he went to the States, but it must be in private, not at a party in view of so many curious eyes.

She finished her bitter lemon and set the empty glass down on the bar counter. Jessica and party had gone, she noticed, so it was safe for her to leave. Rising from her stool, she said, "Thank you for the drink. If you'll excuse me, I'll say good night."

"How do you propose to get home?"

"By taxi. I'm going to phone for one now."

"I'll drive you," he said in an authoritative voice that brooked no argument.

Not that she'd any desire to argue. She enjoyed being helped into her coat, the brief, deliberate touch of his fingers on her bare arm, the casual intimacy of his hand on her elbow as he escorted her out to his car. Tomorrow — who knew? This moment was hers.

Chapter Two

Next morning she woke to a feeling of shivery delight. In her sleep-bemused state it was some moments before she could trace the source of her happiness back to her meeting with Noel Britton the night before.

She refused to accompany him to the party that was being given for Jamie because of her previous involvement with the star, not because of any desire to pique Noel Britton's interest — but she had a strange feeling that by turning down his invitation that was just what she'd done.

If Jessica knew that she'd turned down the chance of going to a very select party and mingling with the famous, not to mention Jamie Gray, she'd say that Lorraine ought to be certified. Just as well she had no intention of telling Jessica about that or . . .

If she didn't make a move she was going to be late for work. She found it difficult to be brisk and orderly with only half a mind, which was all she could give to her various morning tasks: showering, brushing her teeth, getting dressed, making and eating her breakfast of coffee and toast, preparing sandwiches and selecting an apple for her lunch.

The defecting part of her mind was still on last night's dream happening. Had Noel Britton really driven her home? Had his restraining hand prevented her from getting out of the car? Had he taken her into his arms, sliding his hands under her coat, kissing her on the mouth with explosive passion before she could demur? It was effected so quickly and, for all its haste, with such smoothness and expertise that she was knocked off balance. It was like being hit by the rushing force of a tidal wave as she was drawn totally into a kiss that was like none she had ever known. In consequence, the trespass of his hands went unchecked for several seconds. The crazy thing was it didn't seem like the kind of trespass her body had previously objected to and had perfected its own way of dealing with: a frigid backing away that had repulsed the most ardent suitor. Until that moment she hadn't known the meaning of the word ardor. It came as a shock to realize that for the first time in her life she was in a man's arms. In the coffee-break gossip sessions, she had heard the other girls giggling over "losing control" and had thought it very weak-minded of them. Now she knew otherwise. The strength of mind she had prided herself on possessing had only been tested by the callow fumblings of boys. In Noel Britton's hands her flesh yielded and, in body language, asked for more.

"You don't waste much time, do you?" she

had chided, dragging his too-familiar fingers from her breast and tearing from her mind the degrading thought that it had been shaped to fit in his hand.

"Life's too short." His laugh had an undertone of hoarseness that suggested he was not altogether unmoved himself, even though casual sex-play must be commonplace to him. "You're a cool lady. No pretend-hysterics or fake accusations. 'How dare you! This is outrageous!'" he mimicked in the nearest his deep voice could get to a feminine pitch. "Just a firm put-down. You surely can't condemn a guy for trying?"

"No." She'd gone along with that, liking the note of apology in his tone, thinking perhaps that, although it was a routine seduction, the rebuff might be something of a novelty. The majority of girls would be more than willing to dance to whatever tune a man of his exceptional looks and wealth chose to play. On the other hand, she disagreed strongly with his verdict. "Cool lady" was not an apt description.

She had leaned forward, taking hold of his hands for safety's sake, and kissed him on the cheek before saying, "Good night. Thank you for the lift home," and leaping agilely out of the car.

Perhaps, she thought, chewing on the burnt edge of her toast because straying minds and perfect rounds of golden-brown toast are not compatible, that hadn't been very bright of her.

A girl with more guile, a girl with *any* guile, would have hung about to give him the chance to suggest another meeting.

Did she want to see him again? Does a newly hatched chick want to go back into its shell despite the perils it faces in this strange new world? Of course she wanted to see him again!

At lunchtime she ate her sandwich in record time and left the office on the pretext of having some shopping to do. She foiled Jessica's wish to accompany her by saying it was supermarket shopping — bread-and-butter purchases didn't appeal to Jessica — and made the break while her friend's interest was on the wane.

Apart from not wanting Jessica with her in view of what she intended to do, she didn't want another session of how marvelous, wonderful, stupendous and terrific Jamie Gray was up close. Jessica had been so taken with him that she had forgotten to ask her how she had got on with Noel Britton, although she would doubtless remember her lapse. Lorraine knew she could prepare herself for a full-scale interrogation. Jessica — anybody — was welcome to Jamie. The sooner she rid her life of him the better. She could only do this, know it was quite final, by seeing him again.

With this intent, she made for the nearest public telephone box. She set a pile of coins by the coin box and systematically began to dial around the top hotels. Even in his less affluent days Jamie had always had a taste for high

36

living. He had said that he would turn his back forever on second-rate lodging houses and stay only in the best hotels if ever he made it big.

She drew a blank all the way around. Jamie wasn't registered in any of the hotels she tried. As a last resort she decided to phone The Black Cat. She thumbed through the telephone directory for the number and was confused to see several numbers. She dialed the top one and was nonplussed to hear a voice — mercifully female — say, "Mr. Britton's office. This is his secretary speaking. May I help you?" she added when Lorraine didn't speak up.

She ought to have known that the top man would have the top number and supposed she should be grateful that Noel himself hadn't answered.

"I hope so. Could you please tell me where Jamie Gray is staying?"

"I'm sorry. It's against the rules to divulge such information."

"I thought it might be," Lorraine replied resignedly. "I'm not a fan. It's a personal matter, and it's vital that I contact him as soon as possible. You couldn't make an exception, could you?"

"I'm afraid not."

"That's all right," she said flatly. "I understand your predicament and I'm sorry for troubling you."

"Don't ring off," the gentle voice interposed quickly, giving Lorraine cause to wonder if the secretary had read an even more urgent message into her words than was justified. "I'll tell you what I'll do for you. Write a letter to Mr. Gray and send it care of me, Judith Brown, here at The Black Cat. I'll forward it on to him. I have all the information on file, including his forwarding address in the States. It will be no trouble to include your letter because there's bound to be other mail to send on to him. Will that be any help?"

"It's kind of you to suggest it, Miss Brown, and I'm very grateful, but not really. I'd prefer to contact him before he goes to America."

"That's impossible. By now he's halfway across the Atlantic."

He must have gone directly after the party. "I see. Thank you for telling me. I'll see him when he comes back. Thanks again for your kindness. Goodbye." Lorraine put down the phone, feeling warmed by the concern shown by the unknown Miss Judith Brown. She hadn't sounded at all like the sort of young woman she thought Noel would choose for a secretary. Her voice was quite mature. Motherly. Even though her mission had been unsuccessful, she felt inordinately pleased.

It was obvious Miss Brown had jumped to the wrong conclusion, and Lorraine hoped she hadn't worried her. Thank goodness she wasn't in that kind of trouble. Nothing so imperative. This situation had remained static for three years. Another week or so wasn't going to make a lot of difference.

At finishing time she put the dust cover over her typewriter, not without a sense of relief. With so much outside the office to think about, her brain was functioning even less efficiently than usual. Typing wasn't the job she had been trained to do, and, as she didn't seem to have a natural aptitude for it, it required every scrap of her concentration.

She looked up to see Jessica standing by her desk. "Why don't you come to my place to-night, if you've nothing better to do, and listen to my new Jamie Gray record?"

"Another time, perhaps," Lorraine replied. Hoping to soften her refusal, she added, "The truth is, I've got a date with —"

"With Noel Britton? You pulled it off!" Jessica said, anticipating too soon.

"— a sachet of shampoo and a hairdryer," Lorraine corrected.

But when she got home she delayed washing her hair and turned the television sound down so that she wouldn't miss hearing the telephone if it rang. The phone served all the apartments and was situated on the landing one floor below. Normally she wasn't alert for its ring. The absurdity of her hopes brought a faint smile to her lips. Did she honestly think there was the remotest possibility of Noel phoning her?

He had been in her thoughts all day, but it was doubtful that he would even remember her name, let alone wish to see her again. Yet, hearing the sound of the telephone, she still went to her door and hung over the banister rail in silly expectation at least half a dozen times before giving up. Next time it rang she ignored it. She was running the water into the washbasin to wash her hair when someone pounded on her door.

"Telephone for you, Lorraine."

"Thanks," she said, almost wrenching the knob off the door in her haste and racing down the stairs at breakneck speed before making herself slow her pace. It wouldn't do to sound breathless when she answered the phone.

She announced her name and could have wept when an instantly recognizable voice said, "It's me, Lorraine."

"Hello, Aunt Leonora," she said in surprise, because her aunt had phoned the day before to wish her a happy birthday and Lorraine had thanked her for her birthday gift, a matching set of luggage. Was there a hint there that a visit was overdue? Although they kept in touch fairly frequently by phone — about twice a week — her aunt must have something special on her mind to phone her two days in succession. "Lovely to hear from you so soon. Is everything all right?" she asked with a touch of concern.

"It is with me. I was wondering how things were with you. I won't beat about the bush. I've been reading all about Jamie in the morning newspaper, about his going to America and all that. It seems as though he's a big star now to receive such a splash."

"Possibly there wasn't much else of news value. Oh, dear, I didn't mean that in the way it sounded. I'm not vindictive anymore. I'm pleased that Jamie's made it, but that's all I feel."

"I wondered. Only you know if you've got him out of your system for good, and, whether you have or not, reading about him must bring back memories better forgotten."

"I'm all right, Aunt Leonora." It was the truth. Her heart was finally and irrevocably free of him. Even the bitterness had gone. For a long time she had been resentful. She could have saved her own skin. She had actually escaped from the fire unharmed, but she went back to help Jamie. That single action had changed her whole life. She had lost everything: Jamie; a wonderful job that had tested her resources, her energy, her intuition and personal flair to the limit of her capabilities so that she could forget that she got it initially on the merit of her looks. Her present job offered no challenges — and, therefore, no rewards — and she found it tediously boring. But her tediously boring job was not without compensations. Through it she had made friends with Jessica and the other girls, and this had resulted in her meeting with Noel. Was meeting Noel the reason why she no longer felt bitter? "I've seen Jamie —"

"*Seen* him?" her aunt gasped in amazement.

"Not to talk to," she said quickly. "I told you I was going to The Black Cat last night with the girls from the office. What I didn't know was that Jamie was topping the bill. I watched him; I won't say I was unmoved because that would be a lie, but I didn't go to pieces. Afterward, the girls joined the crush waiting to see him. I didn't go with them. I wasn't brave enough to meet Jamie again after all this time with other people present. But I will see Jamie. I've got to talk to him — then it will be over."

"That's my girl," her aunt said in brisk approval, but there was still a faint stirring of anxiety in her voice as she asked, "Any chance of my seeing you in the near future?"

It would make a break, and she always enjoyed her aunt's lively company. She had sufficient days' holiday allowance left — so why the reluctance?

"I rather thought you were saying something when you bought me that gorgeous set of matching suitcases for my birthday. I'll try to make it soon," she promised, hoping her lack of enthusiasm didn't show.

"That will be lovely. Give me some warning and I'll get a few days off work. We can do something, live it up a bit."

It got around to Thursday again.

A full week had passed, with no word from Noel, before she finally admitted to herself that

42

nothing was going to come of their meeting. She ought to have taken advantage of her aunt's invitation.

Ironically, after days of breath-held anticipation, after hesitating before stepping into her bath in case he chose to ring at just that moment and she had to keep him waiting, his phone call roused her from her bed.

"Do you realize it's almost midnight?" she accused when she'd swallowed her first startled reaction that it was Noel phoning her.

"Of course I do," he retaliated sharply. "I've been phoning you on and off all evening. The damn line's been engaged. Who have you been speaking to all this time?"

"No one. The phone is not for my exclusive use. It's a public one that serves all the apartments."

"I never thought of that. What a stupid arrangement."

She felt her mouth curling up at his arrogance, although in honesty she admitted there might be another reason for her smile.

"I want to see you," he announced abruptly. "Can I come over?"

"When?"

"Now, of course."

"Out of the question. Visitors are frowned on at this time of night."

"You'd be better off in jail."

"Hardly. If I were in jail I couldn't get out."

"That's a good point. See you at the main en-

43

trance in ten minutes."

"I didn't mean —" What had she meant if not that? She frowned. "No. It's too late. I have to get up for work in the morning."

"So do I."

"Some people can exist on less sleep than others."

"True," he acknowledged. "Do you eat breakfast?"

"Well — yes."

"Then regard it as an early breakfast. Ten minutes."

"Where are you planning to . . ." It was too late. He'd rung off.

She flew back up the stairs, the question poised in her mind as to where he could be taking her at this time of night unanswered. She slipped out of her dressing gown and dealt with the pearl buttons at the neck of her night-gown, still with little idea of what to wear. Noel was a man of the world. He surely wouldn't expect her to be dressed and made up for a select nightspot in ten minutes? Yet what other type of establishment would be open for meal service at this hour?

The clothes in her wardrobe were sparse. She had preferred to save for quality items rather than spend her money indiscriminately on a jumble of cheaper garments. The gray suit teamed with a glimmer-of-pale-purple silk blouse just scraped by for dressy occasions while not looking out of place in less formal surroundings. She applied her makeup lightly with professional expertise. The trade she had so painstakingly and lovingly learned, and which she had been forced to give up, still had its uses. Usually she complemented the elegance of her suit with a more sophisticated hairstyle, but her hair, conditioned and shampooed earlier in the evening, was as slippery as silk and not to be managed in the few minutes at her disposal. It reached her shoulders, undulating gently to the contours of her face, a shining fall of gold that curved under naturally at the ends. The simplicity of the style gave her face a childish sensuality that was even more disturbing, more potent, than the sophisticated kind which came complete with its own protective hardness.

Checking her appearance, she saw that the flood of hair enhanced the fragility of her features, making her eyes appear larger than they actually were, vulnerable, curious eyes that shone with incredible clarity above the provocative curve of her cheek and the passionate and inviting fullness of her mouth.

She gave a gasp of astonishment. Until that moment of critical analysis, when she tried to see herself as Noel would see her, she had been blind to the picture of wanton enticement her face presented.

She snatched the shining strands back with her fingers, letting them fall loose again when she realized her hair was not responsible for the change. The look was still there. It came from within, born of thoughts she still barely acknowledged in relation to Noel Britton or, indeed, any man. She had never wondered before what it would be like to have the power to torment a man like Noel Britton out of his mind, drive him insane, inflict him with masculine urges he had no will and no wish to deny. She had always thought that girls who, by manner or by dress, set out to lay a trap of seduction deserved to be caught in the snare themselves.

Noel was waiting for her when she got downstairs, his long, lean frame nonchalantly propped against the expensive car parked at the curb. She descended the last few steps, conscious of the tensing of her own body as his eyes ran over it, his steely glance lingering in amused appreciation on the warm awareness coloring her cheeks before contacting her eyes in unmistakable speculation.

He touched her hair. "Nice. It suits you down," he approved, and then he swung open the car door for her to get in.

She hesitated, her breath harsh in her throat. "Where are you taking me?"

Indolently, with no sense of haste, conveying a gesture of lazy possession, his hand curved to her waist. "It can't be your place, so it's got to be mine."

"No." She would have been shocked to know that only her mouth issued the denial; her eyes did not back it up.

46

"I won't push it."

The triumphant sound of his laugh puzzled her too much for her to find appeasement in the seeming capitulation of his words. She looked to his eyes for guidance for her thoughts and saw by the mocking glint in them that he did not think it would be too long before he overcame her scruples and got her into his apartment and, ultimately, into his bed.

To her chagrin she realized the scrutiny was reciprocal and he was also using her eyes to read her mind. She put her hands up to her cheeks in a childish attempt to hide the revealing stain, but it didn't occur to her to veil her eyes by the simple expedient of looking down.

"I thought blushing was a dying virtue," he said, drawing her hand away from her cheek, turning her fully into the beam cast by the street lamp.

"Virtue?" She laughed. "It's a curse."

He lifted her hand, which was still in his keeping, and looked down at her fingers in dedicated thought. She knew, although she had never considered herself to have especially accurate instincts, that he was looking at their ringless state. The burn scars that had once marred them were no longer visible to any but the most discerning eyes.

"Anyone would think that you didn't trust me," he said. "Is it something about me, men in general, or are you taking it out on all men for the misdeeds of one?"

She didn't know about trusting him; she did know it was the first time in three years that she had entrusted her hand into another's clasp without fighting the urge to snatch it away. "Take your pick," she said haughtily in an attempt to cover her confusion. "The price of a meal buys you my company, not my life story."

It was the kind of flip statement Jessica delivered so successfully, always managing to sound intelligent and amusing while making it cuttingly clear to the interrogator that trespass of her privacy was not permitted.

Instead of looking perturbed at being slapped down for prying, he turned the tables on her by applying a mocking note of his own. "You're not like your contemporaries. I would say there are more lurid happenings in the average twelve-year-old's reading matter than have occurred in your life. At your age most girls have lost their virginity. I'll wager that yours is still intact."

"Do you always gamble on long shots?"

"No. I only bet on certainties."

She refrained from further comment. All he could deduce from the return of color to her cheeks was that once again he had succeeded in embarrassing her. It did not confirm that his judgment was correct.

"Forgive me," he said, taking pity on her. "You are so delicious to tease and it's such a novelty. It's a rare thing to find a girl who is so easily shocked."

"I dread to think what kind of girl you usually acquaint yourself with," she replied pedantically.

"Yes — well —" he said, unabashed. "Perhaps the less said about that the better. Let's make a pact. We won't talk about the women I know, and your past life shall likewise be treated as a taboo subject."

Although it was half said in jest, it was also in the nature of a commitment; and, even though it was early days, she knew it was one she wouldn't mind taking seriously.

It was probably just a game to him, but his right hand released her left hand and was then reoffered with formal gravity. "Shake on it." Her right hand went forward, the bargain was sealed and she allowed herself to be directed into the passenger seat of his car.

It was the most luxurious car she had ever been in. The engine made no more than a soothing purr and the suspension smoothed out the bumps so that it was like riding on air. She told herself to make the most of it, because she knew it couldn't last. She was a novelty to him, delicious to tease, a challenge. He couldn't believe that any female was proof against his powers of persuasion, and he was confident that she would succumb. Her resistance would serve as the sweetener that would enhance the taste of victory.

He wasn't trying to hide the fact that he was attracted to her because she was different. At the same time, his intelligent reasoning would tell him it was only a surface difference. Once he got her into bed she would lose her individuality and be like any other girl.

"What are you thinking?" he asked unexpectedly.

Some demon of mischief made her reply with roguish honesty, "I was thinking that, when it gets down to basics, girls are as alike as peas in a pod."

"With one qualification. Some are greener than others," he said, matching her mischief with his quick rejoinder.

The talk continued in this light, inconsequential vein. The atmosphere between them was unstrained, so the superficiality of the conversation didn't matter.

She wasn't conscious of the direction they were taking, only that they were moving at great speed in a strange, monochrome world. The moon had trailed her fingers across the earth, draining it of color and painting everything silver. The stretch of motorway was silver, the steep embankment with its cling of stunted trees was silver, his eyes were silver, the smile on his mouth was silver, untarnished by cynicism or mockery — her thoughts were pure gold.

The speed the car attained so effortlessly was symbolic of the speed with which their relationship was developing. Never in the whole of her life could she remember slipping into such easy compatibility with anyone. If only it didn't have to end. If only it could go on like the road, seemingly forever. But even as the thought rested so lightly on her mind, his foot was easing off the accelerator, preparing to turn off at the next exit point.

He parked the car alongside two giant trucks in the car park of a — transport café.

He queried her look of surprise. "Doesn't it appeal? I'd advise you to reserve judgment until after you've eaten the best steak you've ever tasted in your life."

"Oh, it appeals to me. Very much so. It just doesn't seem to match your lifestyle."

"No. But it matches my humble beginnings."

They had left the car and were walking along the short stretch of rough ground toward the brightly lit, one-story brick and timber building. She was caught off-balance by his last remark. She had thought, by his manner of assurance and authority, that he'd always known great wealth. And yet, on reflection, she wondered why she had arrived at that conclusion. He didn't have that cushioned-from-life, "soft" look about him. The impression she had first formed of him was that he had reached his present comfortable position by his own efforts. He saw what he wanted and he had the tenacity and drive, the determination and — yes! — the ruthlessness to get it for himself.

That led straight into another thought, one which her brain didn't absorb too well. He wanted her. That was as plain as the look in his eye, as the excessive familiarity of his hands when he took her in his arms after driving her home from The Black Cat. He had made a fast play for her, but he had gone back into line without argument when he realized she was not an easy pickup. He was now applying other tactics. He was moving with caution and a kind of smoldering subtleness, but, make no mistake, he still had the same end purpose in mind. He wanted to sleep with her.

Her thoughts stalled as she stubbed her toe on a large stone. If she hadn't lost her footing on the uneven ground, her prim soul shuddered to think where further contemplation would have taken her. Her lost footing took her straight into his arms, which automatically reached out to stop her from falling.

His hold steadied her feet but had the reverse effect on her heart. Its quickened beat gave away her awareness of him. The reaction of her own fingers had been to grab his chest for support. The vibrations under her fingertips told her that hers wasn't the only misbehaving heart. His also was giving away secrets.

Verifying that he never missed an opportunity, his hands moved caressingly down her back, closing briefly on her hips before returning sedately to her waist. His mouth tantalized her lips by brushing over them in the motions of a kiss that was not allowed to materialize. She couldn't tell whether he was paying court to convention, because they could be observed should anyone be looking out of the windows of the transport café, or withholding himself to tease her.

"You can have the rest of that later," he said wickedly, making her think it was the latter.

"Did you have humble beginnings?" she asked, picking up the conversation that had been left trailing before she stumbled, turning her head to look back at him as he held the door open for her to enter the café.

"Very humble. This table all right for you?" he said, indicating one that was near at hand, although they could have had their pick of the room.

Only two of the other tables were occupied by serious diners; a third table housed three burly men in shirt sleeves who looked up briefly as they came in and then resumed their game of cards.

"Yes, perfect."

"T-bone and all the trimmings?"

"Yes, please."

She hoped her thoughts hadn't robbed her of her appetite and wished she'd asked to be let off with just a cup of coffee. She felt too strung up to eat, too conscious of the fact that her life was touching another turning point, too aware that her emotions weren't in the control of her own hands but on strings that were being jerked by this disturbing man. He even seemed to be directing her thoughts.

The waitress came to take their order and then disappeared through the ranch-type swing-door into the kitchen.

Backtracking again, Noel said, not boastfully but without false modesty, "I've got the kind of lifestyle I've always wanted. I've acquired it the hard but satisfying way — by working for it. And yet — want to know something? — the things my parents handed down to me are without price and they are what I value most. Good health, a quick and appreciative eye and a keen brain."

The waitress returned to set two laden oval steak plates before them, another containing chunks of bread, roughly buttered, and thick beakers of strong coffee.

Picking up her knife and fork, she said, "You inherited something more from your parents. You have two very valuable senses: a sense of humor and a sense of proportion."

"I'll go along with that." He reached for the mustard jar and transferred a generous amount to his plate. "They're what keep me on course. The one holds me down to earth, the other stops me from going around the bend."

She pierced a mushroom on the end of her fork. "Your parents — are you lucky enough to — I mean, where are they? Are you a dutiful son and do you keep in touch?"

His eyes took on a shrewd and thoughtful look. "They both enjoy good health and I visit them as often as possible, which perhaps isn't

54

as often as I should. I gather, from your tone, that you are less fortunate?"

"I was still at school when my mother died. I lost my father over three years ago."

"I'm sorry."

"They're reunited now. When my mother died, I think my father was only marking time until he could join her, although he made an effort to pick up the threads of his life for my sake. It must have been difficult for him. All their married life they occupied their own little world to the exclusion of everyone else, and yet they never shut me out, if that makes sense. Somehow my mother saw to it that I was included in their love. It was special. My mother's cool exterior was for the world at large. Her warmth was reserved exclusively for my father; the fire under the snow burned just for him, and he reciprocated her fidelity. I had always leaned toward my mother. When she died, it was inevitable that my father and I became closer." Her expression stilled with reflection. "Life inflicts some bitter blows, but it provides the salve to ease the pain." Her words had a profound ring, the more surprising because of her comparatively young age.

He didn't offer to interrupt, and the compassion of his silence warmed her. It was as though he recognized this as being an extremely rare moment, as, indeed, it was. The death of her parents was something she didn't talk about, and he valued her revelations accordingly.

"Losing my father, after finding him, was especially painful. I had always been a little in awe of him. It took me a long time to realize that he wasn't a godlike being without human flaws, but a man capable of error, a man of great physical and moral strength, and weakness, as demonstrated in the odd lapses when his temper flared out of control —" She stopped abruptly, regaining her own slipping control. "I'm sorry. I can't think what came over me. I didn't mean to sound maudlin. It seems that I have been the one to break our contract, not you. By talking about my past," she explained.

"I'm honored that you could confide in me. You should take the cork out more often. It doesn't do to bottle things up." His grin was wry. "I know it's easier said than done."

She pushed her plate away. "I'm sorry. I can't eat any more. And it is late. I'm going to have great difficulty in getting up for work in the morning."

Without argument he signaled to the waitress that he wanted to pay and took out his wallet. "What kind of work do you do?"

"Office work. Mainly typing."

"Do you enjoy it?"

"No."

"Then why do it?"

"Because I usually pay for my own breakfast."

He handed some notes to the waitress and

shook her hand away when she went to her pocket for the change. "Keep it."

"Thank you, sir. Good night and safe driving," she said, including Lorraine in her wide smile.

As they walked out into the night, his fingers reached out to interlace with hers. "There's more to it, isn't there, Lorraine?"

"Isn't there always," she said grimly. "I was trained as a beauty consultant. I loved my job. I won't be modest about this. I got it initially because of my looks, but I kept it because I was good at it. I was highly thought of by the firm and I was beginning to make a name for myself when —"

She was discovering something nice about Noel. He knew when to remain silent. He didn't put pressure on her to continue. He had the patience to wait for her to take it up in her own time.

"I was in a fire," she said in a voice that stated the bald fact and expressed no emotion. "I was burned rather badly. My hands came off worst. You wouldn't believe how much one's hands are on show. I don't blame a beauty-conscious client for not wanting to buy an expensive cosmetic item that is offered by someone with scarred hands. My employers were very nice about it. They offered to find me something else. I decided I didn't want to be tucked out of sight by them. I preferred to find my own obscurity. I searched around and found it in my present job."

"I knew there was something. I'm forced to ask — what scars? You have lovely hands."

"The scars have gone now, or almost. My hands were badly flawed then. I had to go back to the hospital a great many times. I'm not complaining about that. I was lucky in the surgeon I had. He is a brilliant man. He said the scars would fade, and they have. He gave me his promise that, in time, I would be without blemish."

"There's something inhuman about a person without blemish. It's the little quirks — the faults, if you like — that make a person more endearing. I hope so, anyway, having more faults than most."

"I wouldn't dream of arguing with that," she said emphatically.

"I shall take that as a compliment. Having more faults than most men, I must be proportionately more endearing."

"And conceited, too."

"But not easily sidetracked." They had arrived at his car. He fitted the key in the door lock but did not offer to twist it. "Have all the scars faded, Lorraine? What about the inner ones? Have they gone?"

"Please, I don't want to talk about that. Not yet."

Perhaps never, she added under her breath. Although their relationship had taken giant strides — even in her carefree, gregarious days before the fire, she had never known its like before — she didn't know if she would ever be able to tell him the reason she had lost her confidence and why she found it difficult to trust people. She could not tell it without reviving the bitterness or reliving the horror of that night and the black months following Jamie's defection.

Chapter Three

He drew the car next to the curb at the entrance of her apartment building before he posed the question. "When your father died, was there someone else you could turn to?"

Fearing that he suspected there was a man somewhere in the tangle of her torment, she said, a little wearily, "Aunt Leonora." How much longer could she supply answers without telling him what he really seemed to be asking? "She's a brick. She owns this darling cottage in Kittiwake Bay. It's situated at the end of the town on the edge of the moor; because of its being on higher ground, it has a fantastic view of the sea. I stayed with her when I came out of the hospital. She wanted me to make my home with her permanently — the offer is open any time I care to take it up. It's tempting, but I won't. I had to make my own life, not latch on to hers, and nothing has altered in that respect. We keep in touch by phone and visit each other when we can."

"I'm glad about that. You've had a rough deal — rougher than you're letting on, I suspect. I'm pleased you weren't on your own." He put his arms around her. With that uncanny intuition of his, his kiss was light and undemanding, as if he knew how severely drained she was and that her emotions could take no more. "Good night, sleepy-eyes. I'll phone you."

By unlucky chance he always chose to dial her number when someone else was using the phone. Knowing how much it annoyed him to keep hearing the engaged signal, she was flattered that he persevered until the line was free and he managed to get through to her.

Each time he phoned to ask her out, she accepted the invitation fully expecting it to be the last. It was now four weeks since he'd surprised her by phoning at midnight to take her out for a meal, and he was still surprising her by not losing interest.

He was a wonderful escort, knowing exactly the kind of place she liked to be taken to; but this evening he was mixing business with pleasure. He had booked a table at the Cabana. The cabaret spot featured Toni Carr, an up-and-coming singer he was considering putting under contract.

She decided to wear the white dress, the one she had worn the evening they met. She hadn't worn it since, and, as she took it out of its protective covering and hung it on the outside of her wardrobe, she looked at the dress with a certain fondness. It had marked a turning point in her life.

She applied her makeup with her usual light

but caring hand, shading and blending with subtle expertise to create the natural look which suited her best and did not detract from the loveliness of her green eyes and the delicate shape of her face. She believed that beauty aids should aid beauty and never be allowed to dominate or overpower. She had seen too many girls whose stunning looks were marred by overdoing the makeup. She coiled her hair into a simple chignon, twisting a lock to fall forward onto her forehead from force of habit; there was no longer anything to conceal. Sometimes it was difficult to believe she had been so badly scarred in the fire. Her skin's own natural healing process, plus the skill of a brilliant surgeon, had restored her to her former self. If Jamie saw her now he would have no cause to cringe away from her in horror. She clenched her fingers tightly together and, with effort, put the unhappy memory from her.

Noel was late. That was unlike him. He was always punctual, arriving one minute before the appointed time as though, unlike ordinary mortals, he was above traffic jams or any of the other delaying frustrations that most people have to endure from time to time.

When her doorbell rang she raced to answer it, picking up her coat and evening purse on the way. Opening the door to him, she said, "I was just beginning to wonder what had —" And stopped. To begin with she had to lower her eyes a considerable distance. Even in her highest heels she still had to look up at Noel. But she wasn't looking into Noel's gray eyes. These eyes, not much higher than her own, were a friendly light brown in color.

"Hello, Mr. Peters," she said, recognizing Shane Peters, the compère at The Black Cat.

"Good evening, Miss Marshall."

"Where is Noel?"

"Unavoidably delayed. No cause for alarm. He tried to contact you himself, but apparently your telephone has a peculiar habit of being engaged; he phoned me instead and asked me to relay the message on his behalf."

"I see."

What did she see? The end? She had always known she was too tame, too unspectacular, too uncooperative, to hold Noel's interest for long. Was he bored with her? Had a better prospect turned up and was she being gently set aside?

"It's kind of you to come out of your way to bring the message, Mr. Peters. Thank you for not leaving me in the dark."

"Hang on. You haven't let me finish. It's not kind of me at all; it's my pleasure, even though I am only carrying out the boss's orders. I've been instructed to take you to the club and keep you . . . er . . . suitably entertained until Mr. Britton arrives."

His audacious grin told her that was not quite what Noel had said. "Suitably entertained, Mr. Peters?" she couldn't help teasing.

"All right. His actual wording was, 'Keep your lecherous hands off her. Remember who she is.' "

With a small return of her confidence, she said, "Perhaps I'll just wait quietly here by myself until Mr. Britton can find time to collect me."

"Perhaps you won't. Please, lady. I like my job. You wouldn't have it on your conscience that you'd put me in the unemployment office?"

"Don't tempt me. It might save some other poor, petrified girl from being dragged up onto the stage against her will, as I was."

"Your friends set you up, not me. And don't think too unkindly of them; most girls enjoy the attention. You were the exception and quite the worst case of shyness I've ever seen. I'm sorry for putting you through it." His cheeky smile returned to lighten his eyes. "Anyway, I didn't know you were special to the boss then."

"I wasn't." She wasn't sure she was special to him now. "But for that we probably wouldn't have met. So see what you've got on your conscience."

Flattering as Noel's attention was, it could only end in one way for her — in sorrow. Beneath the sophisticated, figure-hugging white dress beat the crazy, mixed-up heart of a very scared, immature girl. How could she have reached the magical age of twenty-three and feel sixteen in experience and ability to cope?

Some, if not all, of this must have shown on her face, because Shane Peters chuckled richly. "You shouldn't believe all you hear. Sure, the guy's sowed a few wild oats. He's normal, isn't he? But he'd need to be Superman to keep up with all the reports about him."

"You are very loyal, Mr. Peters."

His eyes riveted on her in open admiration. "Shane, if you don't mind. You should be crowing over the conquest, not probing his past as if he were the one on trial and not the —"

He pulled himself up sharply and she took up the sentence for him. "And not the other way around. You think I'm on trial, don't you, Shane?"

"I don't know what to think. Do you mind if we make a move? I might be parked in an illegal area."

He hadn't sidestepped the issue. He honestly didn't know. His first hasty assessment was under review. She didn't know quite how she knew this, since nothing specific in his manner had betrayed him, but he was no longer questioning why Noel was attracted to her, even though she was vastly different from his usual choice of female companion. There had been no shortage of informants to acquaint her with the fact that Noel was reputed to have a rapid turnover of girlfriends. He tended to go for brunettes — tall, sultry, sophisticated yes-girls. Just how long would the novelty of a petite, blonde no-girl last?

At the club, Shane Peters wanted to seat her at the table that was permanently reserved for Noel.

"Please, I'd rather not. Most of the regulars know it's Mr. Britton's table and I'd feel conspicuous. Could you find me a quiet hideaway somewhere?"

"A girl sitting on her own and one with your looks . . . you'd cause a stir wherever I put you. You could wait for Mr. Britton in his office, if you wish."

"I do," she said gratefully. Apart from the privacy it would grant her, she was curious to see where Noel spent his working day.

"I'll get someone to rustle up a cup of tea for you. Unless you'd prefer something more —"

"Tea would be lovely," she cut in. "If it's no trouble."

Shane escorted her to Noel's office and then went to order the tea.

Noel's domain was more opulent than any office she had ever known, in a discreet and expensively tasteful way. Her heels sank into the rich pile of the carpet. Her eyes ran appreciatively over the deep leather armchairs and matching sofa, the oyster-color walls hung with pictures of famous recording artists. Her glance dropped to fix on the leather swivel chair that Noel would occupy when he sat at the wide executive desk with its imposing bank of telephones and a single photo frame containing a picture of . . .

Before she could satisfy her curiosity, Shane returned carrying a tea tray set for one.

"Will you be all right on your own?" he inquired, placing the tray on a small table. "Mr. Britton shouldn't be delayed much longer, and it's almost time for me to open the show."

"Of course. Thank you for the tea."

"If you're quite sure, I'll leave you to pour it yourself. If the boss still hasn't got back, I'll pop in again when I've set things in motion."

Instead of reaching for the silver teapot when he'd gone, she decided to appease her curiosity before her thirst and went around to Noel's side of the desk to look at the photograph. There wasn't a doubt in her mind about the identity of the couple. The man had a tender smile on his face as he looked at the woman. The woman's features were almost a duplication of Noel's in a softer, feminine form. They just had to be his parents. She restored the photo frame to its original position, smiling softly to herself.

There were two more doors apart from the one she'd entered by. One door would undoubtedly give access to his secretary's office, the kindly sounding Miss Judith Brown whom she'd spoken to when she phoned in to try to find out where Jamie was staying. What was behind the other door had her guessing. A private washroom, probably, because there would be occasions when it would be necessary for him to change and freshen up after work before going on somewhere else. She resisted the temptation to find out and poured her tea.

She was finishing her second cup when Noel arrived via one of the mystery doors. He wasn't wearing a jacket and his shirt was immaculate, as if he'd just changed it. His hair was damp and unruly at the front, as if he'd just refreshed himself with a quick wash, more or less confirming that she was right in her surmise.

"Goodness, girl! What are you hiding in here for? Wouldn't you have been happier in the club with some life around you?"

At one time, before she was scarred in the fire, the answer would have been yes. She would have fitted in admirably with the convivial crowd, enjoying their speculation as to how importantly she figured in Noel's life, just as she would have enjoyed being pulled up onto the stage to take part in the birthday celebration spot, which she knew was one of the club's most popular features. In the old days she had reveled in being in the limelight and had mixed easily with people. She hadn't known what it was to be shy, to want to hide oneself away out of sight. The scars had disappeared; there was no need to scuttle into a corner. She remembered the words of the surgeon who had operated on her: "One day you'll walk out of the shadows. You'll find your lost confidence." In time she hoped to prove him right.

She managed to smile up at Noel as she said, "Mr. Peters suggested I sit at your table, but I preferred to wait in here. You've got a lovely office."

"It's a suite, actually, with a mini-flat attached. It isn't as large or as grand as my apartment, but it's sometimes more convenient. I'll take you on a conducted tour," he said, pulling her to her feet and leading her across the room to the door, which he flung open to reveal a smaller office. "This is where my secretary sits."

"I thought that might be Miss Brown's office," she said carelessly, letting the name slip out, her concentration absorbed by the caressing thumb on the tender inside of her wrist.

"How do you know that my secretary is called Miss Brown?"

It was a lightly aired query, and she made more of it by blushing furiously. "You said her name, didn't you?"

"I most assuredly did not."

"Then Shane must have mentioned her name."

"Oh — Shane, is it? Did Shane take you on a conducted tour of these rooms?" he inquired, his eyes narrowing in displeased speculation.

"No, of course not. It wouldn't be his place to do so. He said I could wait in your office and very kindly brought me some tea. Why are you looking at me like that? And why are you cross-examining me?"

"I'm looking at you like this because you are a very beautiful woman. And I'm cross-

69

examining you for the same reason. Shane took a shine to you on the night you went up on stage. Oh, I know he always makes a play for the girls in the birthday spot — that's part of the show. It's expected of him and it gets a laugh. But if I were to find out that he'd repeated his on-stage performance with you, I'd break his neck."

"He was a perfect gentleman. His manner was impeccable. Yours is insulting. Even if he had tried anything, don't you think I would have slapped him down? I'm not attracted to him in that way, and anyway, he's too old for me."

He had the grace, or the subtlety, to look sheepish. "Fair enough. Come on. I'll show you the rest."

Because she was still seething in righteous indignation on Shane's behalf as well as her own — he might be an old roué, but on this occasion he had been grievously misjudged — she allowed herself to be swept into Noel's private quarters. Although he called it a mini-flat, it was comparable to her own apartment in size and considerably more luxurious.

The carpet throughout was a rich chestnut color. The walls were creamy white, except in the tiny bathroom, where mirror tiles were used to create a more spacious effect. A stereophonic music deck took up half of one wall of the main room; the remaining portion of wall accommodated a bar. The floor-length drapes were in the same geometrical pattern as the silk covering of the sofa. In the bedroom, where she found herself before the subtlety of Noel's maneuver occurred to her, the rich chestnut carpet was further enhanced by a magnificent oriental rug. The twist-pleated brown silk wall light extended the full width of the bed and gave out a discreet glow that was kind to her blushes. Being in a bedroom with Noel was not a good idea.

She took a step toward the door, but he took two steps and forestalled her exit.

The welcome that had warmed his eyes when he first came in and saw her cooled to mockery. "Perhaps now I'm glad you chose to wait here in my private suite rather than in full public view. This is cozier. Surely that was the idea?" he said, censuring her backing-away movement.

She gasped. Did he think she had arranged it this way deliberately? Didn't he know she'd been motivated by shyness and a deep disinclination to sit at his table by herself, his reserved table where she would be the subject of gossip?

She said hesitatingly, "I thought you specially wanted to hear Toni Carr sing. If we don't go at once, we'll miss her."

Her chin slid sideways to escape the grasp of his fingers, but she could not evade his eyes as they glided over her body.

His eyes triggered off a reaction wherever they touched. Each part of her body reacted differently, so that it was a different sensation depending on where his eyes rested. His mouth was tight over his lips. Such a sensuous mouth could never go into a hard thin line, but that was the impression it gave. Yet she knew he found her body both sexy and exciting and that he, too, was aroused. His eyes flicked quickly up and down her; all the different sensations combined, and it was more feeling than she could bear. Her skin was burning and yet she felt as though she were being held on ice.

The expression in his eyes was all too readable. He thought he had been good to bide his time for this long. He had seen her presence here as the promise that his patience was going to be rewarded. A promise she was now rescinding.

There was a coldness of purpose about him, a deep-grained resolution that told her more clearly than words that he had no intention of allowing her to escape him.

He said, with icy determination, "I'll take my chance of catching Toni Carr's act another time. That opportunity will undoubtedly present itself again. This one might not."

He had backed away to look at her, but now he stepped closer, close enough for his fingers to slide along her bare shoulder and fiddle meaningfully with the narrow shoulder strap of her white dress.

"No," she said huskily.

"Yes," he said positively.

It was torment not to yield as he meddled

with her shoulder strap in that sensuous, distracting fashion.

"Don't go any further, Noel."

"Why? Will you slap me down as you would have slapped Shane down?"

His malicious teasing brought the color into her cheeks. "Yes."

"For the same reasons?"

"No."

"On this occasion the negative answer is the favorable one. You said you would have discouraged Shane because you weren't attracted to him. May I take it that you are attracted to me?"

"Yes." Her fingernails dug into the palms of her hands. She could not see the crescent imprints but only feel the pain as she said bitingly, "Of course I am. You know I am."

"You also think Shane is too old for you. You are quite right, he is. Am I too old for you? The difference adds up to ten years in actual age, but considerably more in experience."

"I don't think you're too old for me. That's not the reason, either."

"But there is one?"

"Yes."

His face was devoid of expression, not even touched by a flicker of scorn as he said, "It's because I haven't offered to put a ring on your finger."

Perversely, for reasons unknown even to herself, she did not immediately rush to correct his mistaken assumption that she was holding out for marriage. Perhaps, womanlike, she was curious to know how much he was prepared to give up. By her calculations he was thirty-three. To reach that age and still hold his bachelor status, he must place a higher value on his freedom than on any woman he had met. Could his attraction for her tilt the balance the other way? But what thoughts were these? The futility of wasting time on them made her shake her head.

"I couldn't marry you even if you asked me to."

"Couldn't?" That word again. It ruffled him the wrong way and narrowed his eyes in irritation. "Why *couldn't* you?"

"Because . . ." She faltered and lied on inspiration, "I couldn't marry a man I didn't love."

He looked stunned; then he laughed, and she hated him for the superior mockery of his tone. "In that case, I won't complicate things more by asking you to marry me."

He hadn't meant to ask her to marry him, she knew that. He'd spoken in cold jest, little realizing how much it would complicate her situation if he had asked her to become his wife.

His head started to come down. She read the conciliatory expression on his face, but her reactions weren't quick enough to stop her chin jerking aside and deflecting the kiss to her cheek.

"Oh, no, you don't," he said gruffly, claiming

her mouth in savage mastery.

Her brain had been a split second too late in relaying the message that when the conversation turned to marriage, his ardor had cooled. The first kiss had been intended as a token apology before going out as planned to the Cabana to hear Toni Carr sing. In avoiding his kiss she had incited his anger.

The relationship between them was combustible; it always would be. It needed only the smallest thing to set the flames roaring. And, small as her chin was, the gesture of turning it aside was a massive insult to his masculine pride. She knew now that he would never allow her to get away with that.

She had made his blood boil by running away from his kiss. Blood that boils in anger is also the right temperature for passion. She was on the retreat, and this excited him.

Somehow, in her stumbling, naive way, she had found the key to his interest. It was unfortunate that she lacked the adeptness to use it to her own advantage. Man was the hunter, and she brought his hunting instincts to the fore.

He moved in on her with a kiss of wrath that forced her head back into the viselike grip of his hand. The compelling dominance of his hard mouth was a demolishing force that ordered her to submit. His crushing mouth refused her lips the maneuverability to cry out in protest. The hot assault of his mouth . . . the invasion of his hands — one on her neck, the other commanding the small of her back, lining her body along the length of his — made her almost insensible.

She had no fight left in her. She went limp in his arms, a doll who lifted her mouth in docile compliance. But that was not to his liking. He wanted a responsive plaything, and he knew how to get himself one. With undeniable expertise he awoke her own desires. His mouth no longer commanded hers in tyranny, but begged in gentle entreaty.

Her own mouth gained strength and urgency. Her hands were halfway around his neck before a spark of intelligent reasoning warned her of the foolhardiness of her actions.

She had made a mistake in choosing to wait for him in his private suite, giving him a totally wrong impression. This madness that was seizing her now, this desire to stay close in his arms and be taken into rapture by his kisses, was doing nothing to correct his misinterpretation of the situation. It would only seem to confirm that he'd read the message right. He might even think that she had pretended indignation so that he wouldn't think she was too easy, or that she was deliberately playing him along because a woman doesn't like being taken for granted and must be coaxed, not rushed.

How she managed to drag her mouth away from the compelling force of his she would never know. Wanting to go along with the sweetness of the moment, she found it torture to place her hands flat against his chest and gain a little breathing space for herself.

"No!" she gasped.

"No?"

"I can't, Noel. I'm sorry," she said lamely.

"Sorry? You —" The name he had been about to call her was drawn in harshly on his breath. He looked livid enough to commit rape, and his next words told her that he would have felt justified, whatever he did. "All right. This time I'll accept that it's your prerogative to change your mind. But I warn you: if you ever make such a promise again, I'll hold you to it."

"I never made any promise," she denied vehemently.

"Oh, but you did. You promised by implication, and in my book that's just as binding as the spoken word. And don't you forget it. Now, do something with your hair. And your lipstick needs retouching. Let's hope we're not too late to catch the show."

She wasted no time in following his orders. She still felt that she wasn't wholly at fault and that he was just as much to blame for assessing the situation incorrectly. Yet, at the same time, she hadn't expected to be spared. She must guard against such a thing happening again, because next time she wouldn't be let off so lightly.

"Give me five minutes," she said, scooping up her evening purse and disappearing into the bathroom.

Chapter Four

As they claimed their table at the Cabana the cabaret spot was just ending and Toni Carr was blowing kisses to the applauding audience.

With a glint in his eye Noel said, "I hope her voice is as good as the rest of her. Perhaps she'll come back and do an encore."

"Maybe that was the encore," Lorraine speculated dryly.

Toni Carr was certainly a looker. Tall, flamboyant, with the sultry beauty only a brunette can have, she possessed the kind of figure men like best. Ripe curves, long, long legs, fragile wrists, waist and ankles. Her flame was not hidden; it was there in every warm and provocative sway of her lovely body. Her dress, a skintight sheath with a deep side slit, appropriately flame colored, molded to her curves, emphasizing her smoldering sensuality. The back was nonexistent, and the low-cut front was more than suggestive, clinging only to the lower curve of her breasts, revealing most of the upper swell. As she took the final bow, the hopeful wolf whistles told Lorraine that she was not the only one to think that Miss Carr was taking quite a risk.

"Well, well, well! Wouldn't mind handling

her," Noel said, his gray eyes coming around to fix teasingly on Lorraine's face. "In a strictly business capacity, of course."

She refused to let her feelings show. She was well aware of the fact that someone as blatant as Toni Carr would not be to his taste, but the singer would provide a useful weapon to use against her unless she could plot to disarm him. She could steal his ammunition by not letting him know that she was seething underneath, maybe even give him a gentle push in the singer's direction. Seething underneath! She must stop this. She must not allow herself to feel proprietorial toward him.

"Why don't you give her a try?" she suggested casually. "I'm sure if you asked her nicely, she would grant you a private audition."

"In my apartment, you mean? I do have a piano, so it is a feasible proposition."

The rat, he was paying her back in her own coin. "What are you waiting for?"

"Nothing. The manager, who happens to be a buddy of mine, is standing by the bar. I'll get him to pass the message on that I want to see her. I'll invite her to join us for a meal. I won't be long, my sweet. You can study the menu while I'm gone."

Meeting the gleam in his gray eyes, wondering how he could look puckish and scathing at the same time, she said coolly, "Take your time. I'm a slow reader."

She had little interest in the menu. She didn't

care what she ate. It seemed a million years since lunchtime, so perhaps she had got past the idea of food. Her mind was absorbed to capacity by Noel, who was now propping the bar up, deep in conversation with his manager friend. She allowed herself the smallest peep in his direction, knowing any prolonged observation of him would be noticed because his view of her was likewise unobscured.

"Lorraine, my dear, how wonderful to see you. May I join you for a while, just until your escort returns?"

The voice turned her eyes. The kindly face, not exactly handsome but very distinguished looking, transformed her expression, and the warmest smile turned up her mouth and flooded her eyes.

With overflowing joy she said, "Please do sit down for a moment, Sir William. It's good to see you, too."

"How long ago it seems since we last met. And what a transformation!" exclaimed the brilliant surgeon who had given her back her looks. His eyes, a bright paintbox blue, grew warm. "You look fantastic. I saw you come in and I couldn't take my eyes off you. You really are exquisitely beautiful. Tell me, have you regained your confidence?"

"I will. As you told me I would. It's just a matter of time."

"But you've had time. That inhuman, stupid, heartless young scoundrel has a lot to answer for." He pounded his balled fist into the open palm of his hand, and she knew he was wishing that Jamie's jaw was on the receiving end of the punch. "Puny character that he was, I can't even remember his name."

"Jamie. Jamie Gray," she said, her happiness at seeing Sir William again changing into pain at the memory his presence conjured up.

It was not Sir William's fault — he would be the last person to hurt her — but Jamie's face, recoiling from her in horror, lived in her mind; Jamie's voice crying in repugnance, "Oh, my God, Lorraine. No — it's no use. I can't bear to look at you," was haunting close to the surface, needing little resurrection.

Remembering brought back the sensations she had experienced then. The shocked withdrawal, the icy sickness. She pressed her hands to her stomach to calm the waves of nausea. She tried to absolve Jamie by explaining, as if by doing so she might be able to understand it herself. "He couldn't help the way he acted. It was the way he was made. He never could bear anything that was abnormal. He was a natural worshipper of beauty and recoiled from anything that was ugly. I was repulsive to him. It would have been sinful of me to expect him to remain tied to me for life. He was right to run away."

"I agree there would have been no point in his staying. He was too weak to support himself, let along give you moral courage. But I won't have the other. There is no abnormality in being scarred by fire. You were never ugly to me, even at your worst. I remember the day they brought you in, so small and lost and hurt. Even though the flesh was a sorry sight, you had the finest bone structure I'd ever seen. I made a vow to myself to use all the skill the good Lord gave me to give you back the beauty you had once known. And I have. May I?" Without waiting for her permission, he drew back the silky blonde fall of hair from her forehead. "Perfection," he said, excitement stirring his voice. "Sheer perfection." Then he held out his hands. She put hers trustingly in them and smiled as he inspected them minutely before lifting each hand in turn to his lips and kissing her fingers. "No one would ever believe that this skin was grafted," he said with a proud look. "My dear, are you all right?" he asked in quick concern as he noted the bright tears in her eyes.

"I think I'm more all right than I've been for a long time. You operated on me to erase the scars, so perhaps it's fitting that you should be the one to make me take the first step out of the shadows. You're not a phony. You wouldn't tell me that I looked as good as I did before if you didn't think so. And please don't think badly of me. I must sound odiously vain."

"On the contrary, you sound sweetly human. There's an old saying: 'A woman without vanity is like a rose without a scent.' You are a rose *extraordinaire.* You were a little girl pretending to be a woman when we last met. You are a woman now. But I'm deviating. I asked you if you were all right, and you said yes. So why are you crying?"

"Oh, you know me. I was always too emotional."

She stemmed the trembling of her lips. Not for anything would she tell him that he had brought back the bad memories, that for a moment she had been caught in the nightmare terror again.

"My shoulder would be honored to act as a sponge for your tears, but it's not quite the . . . Yes, it is! I see the dancing has started again. How very providential that it's a waltz. My favorite dance. Impossible to gyrate to in that diabolical modern fashion. Will you give me the pleasure of partnering you on the floor, my dear?"

"I'd be delighted." As he took her hand to lead her onto the dance floor she said, "You won't laugh, will you? I fell a little in love with you three years ago. Oh, I know it didn't mean anything and that it's traditional to indulge in fantasies of that nature. Anyway, I played a little scene in my mind where we met again years later and you asked me to dance. You're not laughing, are you?"

"No, my dear," he said as his arm closed around her waist. "I'm not laughing. There were times when I, too, had to make myself remember the doctor-patient ethics of the situation and the fact that you were a married woman."

She stiffened in his arms and her step faltered. "Sir William, when the dance is over I would like you to return with me to my table and stay until my friend returns. I want you to meet him. But please, don't mention that I'm married. By one of life's peculiar quirks, he has a business connection with Jamie. He doesn't know I know Jamie, let alone that I am Jamie's wife."

"You haven't got around to telling him yet?"

"I deliberately withheld the fact from him, just as I have from everyone else. My rings were removed in hospital before the grafting could be done. I never put them back on again and I reverted to my maiden name. That part was easy. I hadn't been married long enough for me to have got used to being called Mrs. Jamie Gray."

"I'm surprised that you are still married." He stopped. "We can't talk about this here. Let's chance your escort's annoyance and go outside. Will you be warm enough without a wrap?" he inquired solicitously.

"Yes," she said.

As she walked by his side she was not unconscious of the fact that he was in fine physical shape. His expensive, well-cut clothes were in the latest fashion. His age — forty-five? fifty? The pure silver of his hair made her add the years, but his youthful face suggested it might be more correct to subtract them.

"Would you consider sitting in my car with me? It's parked just here and we would be assured of privacy."

"After all we've shared? Need you ask, Sir William?"

He had never been attracted to her in that way. If he was being flirtatious with her now, it was because he thought her ego needed the lift.

He guided her toward a silver-gray limousine, in keeping with the luxury afforded by his handsome income. Only when she was cushioned on the soft, red-leather upholstery did he pick up the conversation. "So you are still married, Lorraine?"

"Yes. I ignored your advice."

"When I counseled you to take early steps to end the union, you replied adamantly that there was no point. You said your husband had let you down and you would never give your trust to another man. You also said you could not break the vows you had made to God. I asked if you were prohibited from seeking your freedom on religious grounds. You said no, but that your own principles barred you. Surely, by now, you have had a change of heart?"

"A change of heart, yes — and a change of mind, too. And yet, when I made my vows in church I meant them in all sincerity. I believed then, and still do, that marriage should be 'until death do us part.'"

"The marriage ceremony is cruelly unrealistic. It should be rewritten 'until heartbreak do us part.' I'm deeply concerned about you, Lorraine. It's not just seeing you tonight that has jolted my mind; you have been in my thoughts for a long time. I've regretted not keeping in touch with you. I've restored the looks of many pretty girls, but you are the first one I've ever allowed myself to feel personally involved with. When you walked into the restaurant tonight, you walked back into my life. I promise not to trouble you or embarrass you; I simply want to be your friend. I won't lose track of you again. Take this card with my home address and private telephone number on it and put it away. Promise me that you will use it if you need help."

"I promise," she said, closing her fingers around the card.

Sir William flicked on the interior light. "Your address, please, and telephone number if you have one."

It had the ring of a command and she obeyed, watching the hand that so firmly and precisely wielded a scalpel write the information down in a distinctive, flowing script.

He turned out the light. "I must return you or your escort will be out for my blood. One thing before we go back. I have taken dreadful liberties with your body in the course of my work. You are no longer my patient. This liberty is for me." He bent his head and kissed her, very expertly and pleasantly, on the lips. "Medical ethics no longer apply. Only you can say whether or not that liberty was permissible."

There was no one she owed more to or held more dear in her heart. She found his words touchingly old-fashioned and replied by returning his kiss, brushing her lips across his cheek and not his mouth. "Dear Sir William, I'm so pleased we've met again. I badly need a friend, someone I can talk to freely. So much has been bottled up in me for so long. Do you know what I mean?"

"Perfectly." His arm removed itself from her shoulder. "Come, my dear."

She had hoped that she might discreetly excuse herself and slip into the powder room to retouch her makeup, smooth her hair and generally remove the evidence of the emotional scene she'd had with Sir William before introducing the two men, but she saw, with a sinking heart, that Noel was already sitting at their table. As she could not let Sir William go up and introduce himself, she could only hope that she did not look as disheveled as she felt.

As she approached, bringing Sir William in her wake, her heart dropped further when she saw Noel's strained expression. His mood had been dark enough before, but it was obvious that it had suffered a sharp deterioration in the time she had been absent. The fact that Toni Carr wasn't with him made her wonder if his mission had been unsuccessful. Was the singer piqued because he hadn't arrived in time to see her performance? Had she refused to join him at his table? That could certainly account for his ill temper.

"I'd like you to meet a friend of mine," she said as Noel rose to his feet, her expression making an appeal for him to like Sir William. No answering warmth came to his eyes, and an involuntary shiver went through her body as she said with proper deference, "Sir William, may I introduce Noel Britton to you? Noel — Sir William Vane. Sir William is one of our most eminent surgeons in the field of plastic surgery. I owe the fact that I am not badly scarred to him."

"Your own healthy skin did more to aid your recovery than I did," he said before turning to Noel. "How do you do?"

Sir William had a penetrating way of looking at a person, perhaps something to do with the nature of his work, as if he were stripping away the face that was presented to him and probing what lay underneath. It could be disturbing.

Not only did Noel meet the shrewd blue eyes unflinchingly, but Sir William's scrutiny was matched with equal keenness as he extended his hand. "How do you do, sir? Will you join us?"

His manner was too civil, too formal. She didn't know what it did to Sir William, but it chilled her.

"I have already been absent from my own party for too long," Sir William said pleasantly enough, despite the slight frown which touched his brow.

It was not the happiest of remarks, because it drew attention to the fact that she had been absent for the same length of time. The narrowing of Noel's eyes told her that the same thought had gone through his mind.

"Then surely a few more moments will make little difference one way or the other?" he said.

The words were all right; it was the tone that was wrong. This was no friendly entreaty but a command. Didn't he appreciate the importance of Sir William's position?

She didn't think Sir William would bend, even to a will as strong as Noel's, but she was wrong.

He nodded and said, "That makes sense."

Noel snapped his fingers to alert a circulating waiter and had an extra chair brought over. He detained the waiter while he inquired what Sir William would have to drink.

"Thank you, that is most kind. However, I can't let you have your own way in this," Sir William replied, the charm of his smile sufficient to eradicate the offense which Noel might have taken at the refusal. "I am abstaining this evening because I am in the operating theater tomorrow, but please don't let me spoil your pleasure. Order for yourselves."

"Far be it from me to lead you into bad

ways," Noel drawled, conceding the point, but not in a nice way.

There was a hint of mockery in his voice that scorned such worthiness, but, to Lorraine's mind, it did not ring true; Noel was moderate in such things himself. He was a social drinker. The well-stocked bar he kept was for the entertainment of his associates and friends, and he made it a golden rule never to touch liquor while conducting business because he believed in the virtue of keeping a clear head.

"What will you have, Lorraine? Your usual?"

Under normal circumstances she would have said yes and let him order a bitter lemon for her, knowing that he would order wine with their meal, but she was finding enough bitterness to swallow in the way he was talking down to Sir William.

She said sharply, "Nothing for me just now, thank you."

Noel's left eyebrow lifted derisively. "It seems that I am drinking alone. I always think solitary drinking is so decadent," he said, his mouth closing in relish round each word before turning to the waiter. "A whisky and American dry."

Had they been on their own, she would have said, "Why not make it a double? What's decadence if it's not doubled?"

Had he lifted the thought from her mind? With sickening clarity she heard him instruct the waiter, "Make that a double."

She knew that his eyes were challenging her to comment. She tightened her mouth. The situation was bad enough as it was. She didn't want Sir William to get caught in the crossfire of their angry words.

Sir William said blandly, maybe trying to smooth things over but really making them worse, "You didn't get here in time to see the show?"

There was a taut silence. Then Noel's lips parted in a brittle, barbed smile. "Unfortunately, no. We were . . . delayed."

The studied pause, deliberately inserted to revive in her mind the reason for the delay, brought the shameful rush of color to her cheeks.

Ignoring Noel, aiming at normality, she said, "Was Toni Carr good, Sir William?"

"The audience thought so, and I must admit she's not hard on the eyes and she has quite a pleasant voice."

"It was unfortunate we couldn't get here sooner . . ." Her voice trailed off. It might be imprudent to say that Noel was thinking of signing Miss Carr up. Perhaps these things were conducted in secrecy.

The conversation, severely hampered by Noel's mood, never lifted, and it was hard going all the way.

She was fuming. Because Jamie had turned out to be so weak, Sir William thought she was a bad judge of character, a risk to herself. She realized now that she had asked Sir William to come back to meet Noel not merely for reasons of convention, but also as a piece of self-indulgence. Foolish of her, as things had turned out, but she had actually wanted to prove to Sir William that she was capable of knowing a man of charm and stability. Noel's manner was charm*less*. She was seeing a side of him tonight that she had never seen before. He wasn't making up for Jamie; he was underlining the fact that she had no insight about people and attracted the worst possible types.

Pulses were beating painfully in her head. Disappointment and tension had a drying, strangling effect on her throat. And if she had to persevere with the smile on her lips for very much longer, it would crack.

It came as an infinite relief to hear Sir William say, "And now I really must go. I'm glad to have met you, Britton." Turning to Lorraine, he said, "Convey my warmest regards to your delightful aunt."

"I will, Sir William. Aunt Leonora will be pleased you remembered her."

Taking her hand in his, Sir William bent over it and said softly, for her ears alone, "I meant every word I said earlier. I'll be in touch." His lips graced her hand with a kiss. He straightened and turned on his heel, threading his way through the tables in search of his own.

She switched her eyes to look at Noel. Tense with anger, she fully expected that by this time he would be having second thoughts about his appalling rudeness, and she wasn't going to give him the satisfaction of apologizing to her before she'd told him exactly what she thought of him.

He forestalled her outburst. His eyes were gray points of steel, impaling her, piercing her to the marrow. Through gritted teeth, he said, "Don't ever do that to me again. I will not tolerate such treatment. When I take a lady out I do not expect her to desert me for some silver-tongued Lothario. Kissing your hand! Fawning over you!"

She was almost too stunned to take in what he was saying. She had to digest the words slowly, and then a look of incredulity came to her face.

"You must be out of your mind if you think Sir William's interest in me is anything but professional. I'm just an ex-patient to him. A case on his files."

"I notice you said *ex*-patient. Does that make it ethical? Don't belittle my intelligence by looking at me as though I am insulting your integrity. You're not so naive that you don't know when a man fancies you."

"Fancies me? Sir William?"

"Yes, your precious Sir William."

"That is an ugly and utterly preposterous speculation to make."

"Hardly a speculation. Lust overlaid every look he sidled your way."

She gasped in desolation. "There was nothing sneaky or lecherous about the way he looked at me. I'll never forgive you for saying such a thing. For spoiling a very special relationship for me, or trying to, because I won't let your warped mind make any difference. When I was in a desperate way, when my reason as well as my life hung on a thread, Sir William proved himself to be my friend, and you don't know how scarce friends were at the time. He didn't just give me back my looks; he gave me my will to live. I owe him my life."

"Don't think he doesn't know that, or that he won't use it to extract suitable payment. If he hasn't already started dropping the odd hint, he'll soon be pointing out ways for you to express your gratitude."

"I hope you are not suggesting what I think you are. You are so wrong, Noel."

"Am I?" His left eyebrow quirked and held that position.

Damn the man. He could say more with his speaking eyebrow — convey more sarcasm — than a whole string of carefully thought-out words could express. "You are wrong," she repeated miserably. "It's not like that."

"Are you telling me that when he took you outside he didn't make a pass at you?"

"That's exactly what I am telling you."

"Then who smudged your lipstick? Do you still insist that he didn't kiss you?"

"No . . . yes . . . he was comforting me. It was

innocent. And anyway," she said, letting fly as her temper surged out of control, "whether it was or not is none of your business. It has nothing to do with you."

"It has everything to do with me. You are with me, and that makes it my business." His fingers fastened so fiercely around her wrist that she wondered why it didn't break, yet she closed her mind to the pain. Excruciating though it was, she would not give him the satisfaction of knowing that he was hurting her.

She had awakened a fiend. His reaction was . . . what? She shook her head as though trying to understand his motives. She had believed that he was in a foul mood because he'd missed Toni Carr's performance, because his attempt to arrange a meeting with the singer had met with no success. His violent manner suggested something deeper. She looked down at her wrist, still bound by his possessive fury. That was the word she was seeking. Possessive. His reaction was possessive.

It was because of the bond she shared with Sir William, the esteem and affection they felt for one another. Noel did not understand. How could he? He knew she had suffered burns in a fire. She hadn't told him the depth of her suffering. He didn't see Sir William through her eyes. He looked at him and saw a rival. Noel was . . . could he be . . . jealous?

She didn't know which stunned her most, the fact that he saw Sir William as a serious contender or that he cared enough to mind.

She sat back suddenly and her anger left her.

He said, as though unable to let the subject drop, "Your precious Sir William was eating you with his eyes."

Her quick wit replied for her so that she did not have to take her mind too far from the absorbing realization she had come to. "That's better than slaughtering me with his eyebrows. I've lost my appetite," she said, pushing the menu away.

His eyebrows expressed amusement at the reference to them; her reluctance to eat met a brick wall opposition. "You'll eat. Make your choice," he said menacingly.

He had misunderstood her words. It was not temper that had stolen her appetite but surprise at his caring. Jealousy was never commendable; but if he cared, she could forgive him worse faults than that. If he cared enough she could forgive him anything. If he cared . . .

How did one know? She should have left well enough alone. Further thought was destructive. Was his heart affected, or his pride?

"Decide," he said, stabbing the menu with a blunt finger. "Or I'll decide for you."

"I won't be talked to in this dictatorial manner. I am not a child."

"Only when it suits you."

"What's that supposed to mean?"

"You know when to draw back behind maidenly virtue. I'm wondering which face you put on for your fawning friend."

Her short-lived happiness deserted her. Noel had obviously convinced himself that Sir William was out to seduce her. He didn't care about her — only the conquest. He couldn't bear to think that another man might succeed where he had failed.

"I refuse to stay here to be insulted." Although she was quaking inside, no one would have guessed from her sharply raised chin and her bright, challenging eyes. "I'm going home. I don't expect you to take me. I'll call a taxi."

"You would, too! If I let you. After spending half the evening smooching on the dance floor with another man and going outside with him and doing goodness knows what — although I doubt if goodness had anything to do with it — you'd walk out and leave me. I'm not going to let you. You'll stay, you'll eat, you'll dance with me — to my tune. Your conduct has attracted too much attention as it is."

If she had needed further proof, there it was. He didn't care about her. All he cared about was his pride. He wasn't going to have people say about him, "Did you see that blonde walk out on Noel Britton?"

She was more shattered for having held the belief, even for so short a time, that he might care about her. It had been wishful thinking on her part. Instead of pandering to the endless ache inside her that had grasped at the smallest indication that he might return her feelings, she should have remembered the way he held her in his arms earlier in the evening. There had been no burning love in his ardor, no tender commitment for the future. There had been wrath in his kiss where gentleness should have been. It all went back to the fact that she had been foolish enough to wait for him in the privacy of his suite. She should have known what he would make of that. He hadn't forgiven her for — how had he worded it? — drawing back behind maidenly virtue. She hadn't got off lightly at all, as she had imagined, but had only been granted a temporary respite. Whatever he set his sights on he pursued with relentless tenacity and ruthless determination. Not knowing when to give up was the secret of his success. He wanted her; he wouldn't rest in his efforts until he got her.

She dragged up eyelids that felt heavy enough to have been embedded in cement and looked at Noel's strong, egotistical, handsome face and wondered how she was going to protect herself. Strangely enough not from him — from herself.

Her own feelings would destroy her. Knowing where she stood with him didn't change a thing. She was like her mother. The fire under the snow burned for just one man. So help her, for him.

Chapter Five

"I'll skip the appetizer and have tarragon chicken, then profiteroles," she said, banishing the tremble in her lower lip and managing a reasonably composed voice.

"Sounds all right. I'm a soup, steak, cheese and biscuits man myself."

He ordered two bottles of wine: a deep golden sauterne to complement her chicken, a full-bodied claret for himself.

She realized there was some justification for his annoyance. Now that she was cooler she admitted to herself that he had spoken the truth when he said her conduct was attracting too much attention. Even when her anger was in full spate she had tried — admittedly not very successfully — to keep her voice low, aware that they were in a public place and receiving more than their share of notice. Still, she was not really the one responsible for the undue attention they were receiving. If Noel hadn't been so well known, if they'd just been any man and a girl out on a date, the quarrel would have been smiled upon as a lovers' tiff.

Noel wouldn't forget the embarrassment she had caused him or easily forgive her for it. She regretted her part of it and could see his point and, also, where she had gone wrong. No escort likes his companion of the evening to go off with another man. Dancing with Sir William might have been barely permissible; to go outside with him was not. Someone was certain to have observed them, as Noel was all too well aware. Little wonder that he was annoyed with her.

She did not blame herself for being joyful at seeing Sir William again after so much time, but when he had asked if he could join her, she ought to have had the subtlety to explain that she didn't think it was such a good idea but that she would be delighted to meet him at any other time he suggested.

Oh, for discretion and hindsight! Because she had lacked both, Noel had retaliated with accusations and slurs that were too hurtful to be ignored. They had called for immediate repudiation. She'd had to tell him he was wrong about Sir William.

Biting hard on her lips, she said in contrition, "I really am sorry, Noel. I stand by what I've said, but I agree that it should not have been said right here. I'm sorry I let the situation get out of hand. I should have put Sir William off and arranged to meet him at some other time. I share your distaste of making a spectacle of myself in public."

A nerve jumped in his cheek, a violent involuntary contraction that matched his savage expression. He shrugged in a way that suggested he was giving himself a mental shake, and almost immediately his eyes glazed over with indifference. "Forget it. Let's say we both got a bit carried away."

In self-protection her eyes dropped to her plate. The words were conciliatory, but his delivery of them slapped her down. If she had been needled by his anger, she was insulted by the indifference, the disinterest, that had replaced it.

She concentrated on her food. The chicken in its delectable sauce was unequaled in taste. It was uncomplimentary to the chef to eat such exquisite fare with such dogged determination.

They had ordered late. They were among the last to eat, and by the time they reached the coffee stage the restaurant was beginning to acquire an empty look, although the group was still playing for anyone who was inclined to dance. The couples on the floor were dancing in traditional ballroom style. Lorraine was more used to the improvisation of disco dancing, although she liked to watch couples who could dance well, particularly when they did the deliciously lighthearted Latin-American dances such as the samba and the cha-cha. She regretted the fact that she had never had the opportunity of mastering the steps herself. That being so, she hoped Noel would forget his threat to make her dance with him, though she had to admit her feelings on the subject were complex. She both dreaded, and was filled with an insane longing, to go into his arms.

Had her face revealed more than it should? There was an odd smile on his mouth — a smile? a sneer? — as his gray eyes rested on her in open contemplation. Steel is hard and gray is cold, and his steel-gray eyes were both hard and cold, yet they left her in no doubt of what he was contemplating. His glance never left her face, and still it stroked every inch of her body into sensuous response.

"I'll have that dance now," he said.

He came around to her side of the table. She rose to her feet, knowing it was wiser to accept his dictum. Any protest would be brushed aside. He walked behind her; his hands fitted to either side of her waist as he propelled her forward. On reaching the space of floor set apart for dancing, he turned her fully into his arms. She was oblivious to the beat of the music; she could not hear it above the beat of her own heart. He regarded her with those narrowed, metallic eyes and, even though he held her in correct ballroom position, it never occurred to her that her feet should be in motion until his foot moved forward, forcing hers back in automatic retreat.

"I should have told you. I can't dance," she said defiantly.

"You were doing all right earlier on. Relax and follow my lead. I presume that's what Sir William said when you told him you couldn't dance."

"It didn't occur to me to mention it to him," she replied with startling truthfulness. "I knew he would guide me correctly."

"Don't I merit the same kind of trust? Or is it that you can't abide to be in any situation that puts you under my dominance? In this kind of dancing, man sets the pace, woman submits to his will. Perhaps you would prefer it if we danced disco style — the ultimate free-for-all, where neither partner takes the lead and each does his or her own thing and hopes that it will be compatible."

She must not let him draw her. "You don't think skill comes into disco dancing at all, then?"

"It's not skill that's lacking, but subtlety," he responded.

In a less recalcitrant mood she would have found him easier to follow than Sir William. His steps were stronger, his guiding arm more forceful, the pressure of his fingers on her back giving gentle indications of what came next. It would have been no effort to follow his movements and glide naturally along to the slow, sweet beat of the music. It was more of an effort to hold herself aloof in anger at his taunting.

He announced abruptly, "For once I agree with you. You can't dance. You should not look at your feet, even if it does provide an excellent excuse for not looking at me."

Everything she did or said seemed to be

viewed in his eyes as a deliberate act of provocation. Earlier, when she had chosen to wait for him in his suite, he had assumed she was asking to be seduced. Now, as she pretended undue absorption with her feet so as to keep some distance between them, he took her action as an offense. It was as if he had to exert complete mastery over her by pulling her more firmly into his arms and increasing his hold on her. She felt her stomach muscles tauten as their bodies touched.

"You're too stiff," he said. It was not a reprimand but a jeer, because he knew her reserve was caused by his nearness. His voice whispered insidiously in her ear, "Let your body go. Just sway to the rhythm. Allow your legs to move freely from the hips."

"I didn't realize you were such an expert."

"I'm not. I just hold the opinion that everything worth doing is worth doing well. Did you know that dancing was one of mankind's earliest forms of expression? Dancing is older than anything except eating and drinking and . . . Can you guess what else has survived the years and will continue to do so as long as people exist?" He smiled when she didn't answer. "Of course, you know how primitive man gave his emotions an outlet when he banked up the fire and crawled under the animal skins onto his bed of twigs and dry grass next to his mate."

She purposely ignored the allusion to lovemaking and said, "I didn't realize dancing dated back that far."

"It came before speech. Language, as we know it, hadn't been thought of when our Stone Age counterpart was drawing, on the walls of his cave, not only the animals he hunted with his crude flint axes — bison, wild boar, deer and elk — but also scenes depicting the rhythmic outlet of his thoughts and emotions."

She was mesmerized by the thought that people had been dancing before the Christian era and had danced down through the centuries ever since. It was not just a vogue; it was a form of expression intrinsic to life.

As her mind relaxed, the slow fascination of the rhythm took over her feet and she could even speak without stumbling. She was quite disappointed when he said it was time to take her home. She realized with surprise that they were the only couple on the floor.

"Thank you for the dancing lesson," she said sincerely. "I enjoyed it."

He looked down at her for a moment, his expression still. Then he smiled, and it was a smile of such rare charm, one she had never seen on his face until that moment, that she almost started back in amazement. "So did I," he said. "We must do it again some time."

This kinder mood lasted on the journey home. He parked the car just short of the pool of light cast by the street lamp outside her apartment building.

In the light available she could just see that his eyes were still benign as he said, "I wish I understood you, Lorraine. I might if I *knew*. I know you have a past — everyone has. I'm sure yours is as white as virgin snow compared with mine. The muddy patches in my past don't bother me. Yet this thing in your past obviously bothers you."

It wasn't difficult to know what had brought this on. A piece of her past had walked in on her tonight in the form of Sir William.

"Yes, it bothers me," she said guardedly.

"So far you've only given me the headlines — the bulletin announcements, as it were — but never the details."

At the beginning she hadn't told him because it had seemed pointless to put herself through the ordeal, believing as she had that nothing could come of their friendship. But perhaps now the situation had altered. He hadn't grown tired of her and showed no signs of doing so. As things stood at present, she owed it to him to tell him.

If only she could know for sure his motive in wanting to know. If it was to even up the score with Sir William, because in his supreme conceit he couldn't bear to think that any man knew things about her that he didn't, then she owed him nothing.

What did it matter whether she owed it to him or not? Eventually she would have to tell him. Preferably before he found out, which he undoubtedly would when Jamie returned from the States.

It was going to be tricky. She must try not to discredit Jamie too much. She didn't want to cause bad feeling between the two men. And she must make him promise not to take up the battle for her. Not that she anticipated one. Jamie would be glad of his freedom now that he was a big star. She wondered why he hadn't sought her out to ask her to be released from their marriage before now. This wasn't a new thought. It was one she had puzzled over before. Perhaps Jamie had been too busy chasing success to take time off to put his private life in order.

Noel's voice broke into her thoughts. "Do you remember the first time I took you out? I called you on the telephone, at an unpardonably late hour, and we drove out to that transport café for a meal. You let your hair down that night."

She knew he was speaking figuratively and that he was referring to the way she'd talked about her early life, about her parents and the very special love they'd had for each other. She had shared thoughts and feelings with him that had been kept guarded from everyone else. Just thinking about the way she had, to use his expression, "let her hair down" brought a lump to her throat. It still touched and surprised her that she'd known such instant rapport with a stranger.

To buy herself a few moments' time in which to compose herself, she pretended to take him literally. "I'd just washed it," she said, brushing her fingers against her hair. "It was too soft to put in a chignon in the short time you gave me to get ready."

His tone held gentle rebuke. "You know that's not what I meant. You told me a lot about your past that night. You even surprised yourself. Characteristically, you're a very self-contained, private sort of person. Yes?"

"Yes," she agreed gruffly.

"You told me you had been in a fire. In consequence you lost your job because it was thought that the top-drawer customers you sold top-drawer-priced beauty aids to might object to your disfigured hands. Your hands are no longer disfigured. The surface scars have gone. I asked you about the inner scars. I asked if they had faded and you said you didn't want to talk about it. Do you feel like talking about it now?"

He was making it easy for her. Once she got over the difficult hurdle of the opening words, she would be all right.

He said, both perceptively and persuasively, "It's important to us that you tell me. Something that happened then, during the fire or in the circumstances surrounding it, is keeping us apart. Am I right?"

"Yes." She nodded her head so fiercely that the key hairpins in her hair lost anchorage and proved inadequate to the task of supporting the weight of her chignon.

The silky, pale-gold rope slowly unwound and collapsed totally as he removed the remaining hairpins. "Oh, God, how much I've wanted to do that — how much I want you. I'm obsessed by you. It's beyond endurance. I've got a monomaniacal hunger for you that's burning me up. Your hair is so beautiful, as fine as spun gold," he said, gathering it in his hands and caressing the strands. "I love it however you arrange it, but I like it this way best. Ever since that first date when you 'let your hair down' in more ways than one, I've dreamed of waking up and finding it straying across my pillow."

The restless caress of his fingers combing through her hair stirred up a frenzy in her breast. She knew she should hold herself aloof, ignore the dangerous sensations he aroused in her. How could she control the thoughts in her head when his fingers were tormenting and delighting every part of her scalp?

"Promise me you'll never cut your hair. Always keep it long. If only I could climb up it, like the prince in the fairy tale, and storm your impenetrable tower. I've tried to be patient, but if you don't give in soon I think I'll go crazy."

"Rapunzel," the Grimms' poignant tale of bitter realism, had always been a particular favorite with Lorraine. But no smile of tender memory touched her lips, because suddenly she had come to her senses. If she'd had a pair of scissors in her hands at that moment she would have emulated the witch's actions in the fairy tale. With a snip, snap she would have cut off her tresses just to spite him. The prince had loved Rapunzel to distraction; he had asked her to be his wife. Noel had not owned to love, only lust. And he had not asked her to be his wife, only his bedmate.

She thanked God for her long hair, knowing that it had saved her from making a fool of herself. Seeing it gently uncoil had triggered off something in him. Until that moment he had moved so slowly, so cunningly and cautiously, inviting her confidence with his treacherous sweetness and kindness. He had fooled her so completely that she had been tripping over herself to tell him everything. Her lack of eloquence, her inability to conjure up the right words, had been a blessing for once, a timely hindrance.

His patience with her on the dance floor, his persuasive sympathy as he encouraged her to talk about the fire just now — they were deliberate ploys to soften her up. Thank goodness his sweet-talking trickery had come to light. He didn't care about what had happened to her; all he cared about was what he wanted to happen now. He didn't want to even the score with Sir William; he wanted to beat him. He wanted to get to her first.

She dragged her hair from his fingers, ignoring the searing pain in her head as he proved reluctant to relinquish his hold. "The next act has just been rewritten. The big seduction scene is out. My hair will never stray across your pillow," she said with a vehemence that matched the raging fury of her thoughts. "I'll cut it off first."

"What's brought this on?" For a split second her attack stunned him, delaying the angry retaliation. The bite was back in his voice as he said, "You reverse moods quicker than any female I know."

"And you're an authority on females, aren't you? The expert. For all your skill and dexterity in handling them, you haven't had much luck this evening. First Toni Carr, then me."

"What do you mean by that?" he demanded.

"No doubt your friend, the manager of the Cabana, passed on your message inviting Miss Carr to join us for a meal. Your sultry songbird didn't join us, so obviously she turned down your invitation. Isn't that so?" She smirked sweetly.

"If you are suggesting that Miss Carr viewed the prospect of my company with distaste, then no, it is not so. She had another booking. It's not unusual for a relatively unknown singer, struggling to make a name for herself, to have a taxi waiting to whisk her to a second engagement. That was the predicament Toni Carr was in this evening. She asked for a rain check. I'm taking her out for a meal tomorrow."

"Good. I hope the evening lives up to your expectations."

"Who said anything about evening? She works then, remember? I'm taking her to lunch."

"And then back to your apartment for a private audition?"

"Probably. Jealous?" he taunted. "You don't have to be. I'm taking you out tomorrow evening. So whether it lives up to my expectations rests entirely with you."

Oh, no! She couldn't stand it. How much more could she take? She knew that he would work on her until she gave in. Each time they met she was finding it more difficult to resist.

If only she could get away somewhere, away from his devious charm and his disturbing influence. She must have time to herself. She owed it to herself not to be browbeaten into anything. If she could get away from him for a while she would have a chance to think, and she might also be able to build up some reserves of strength.

"I'll call for you at the usual time," he said.

"No." Even though she closed her eyes in despair, her no rang out emphatically.

"No?" he challenged.

"Did I forget to tell you? I won't be here. I'm —" Her brain was spinning wildly. "I'm going to Aunt Leonora's tomorrow. I'm finally paying her that overdue visit."

"Is this the truth, Lorraine?"

Her brain might have spun an inventive lie in the first place, but she could make it the truth by going in to work tomorrow and making arrangements to take a week's holiday. She could leave for Kittiwake Bay on the evening train.

"Yes, it's the truth."

Perhaps she had taken too long in replying. Frowning deeply, he said, "You wouldn't lie to me, would you? It isn't that you've arranged to go out with Sir William tomorrow?"

"No, I haven't arranged to see him tomorrow. I'm catching the seven o'clock train for Kittiwake Bay."

Her cheeks were burning. Deception was a game some people played with ease, but not Lorraine. She prayed that he wouldn't ask any awkward questions, such as was she going by prior arrangement or was it a newly reached decision. He was shrewd enough to have realized that although she wasn't lying, neither was she telling the whole truth.

"How long will you be away?"

"A week."

"I'll call you," he said.

His tone was disturbingly cool, but at least she wasn't going to be made to talk herself into further trouble, which was what she seemed to do every time she opened her mouth.

She got out of the car, lifted her hand in a goodbye gesture and walked quickly away. He waited until she was safely inside, as he always did, before driving off.

She met with no opposition at work. She was granted a week's holiday leave to commence the following day. She phoned her aunt to let her know of her sudden decision to visit and was warmed by the happiness in Leonora's voice as she said it was the best news she'd had all day and how much she was looking forward to having Lorraine with her.

As she packed the simple things she'd need, taking only the barest necessities, Lorraine knew the feeling was reciprocal. A surge of homesickness had entered her blood, and she couldn't wait to be there.

She was moving at great haste, with not a lot of time to spare, when her doorbell rang. She would have to get rid of whoever was there quickly or she would miss her train.

She couldn't believe it when she opened the door and found Noel standing outside her apartment.

"I can't stop now," she said in desperation. "I'm in danger of missing my train as it is."

"Miss it," he commanded. "That's why I'm here. I'm driving you."

Driving me crazy, she thought. "Why?" she gasped.

"I could do with a breath of sea air. You're not the only one who needs a break. I can't remember the last time I had a holiday, although I've traveled extensively, taking in all the exotic holiday spots. It's always business first, with a pair of swimming trunks tucked into my suitcase in the vain hope that I might have time to use them."

"Unless there is an unscheduled heat wave, which is very unlikely, you won't get to use your swimming trunks at Kittiwake Bay. It's the coldest, breeziest bit of English coast there is, although bracing is what my aunt calls it. But why do you want to go there? Or — wait a minute — perhaps I'm presuming too much. Perhaps you intend to drive me there, drop me off, and then go somewhere else?" she said hopefully.

"No. Kittiwake Bay sounds nice to me."

"But — why Kittiwake Bay?"

"Because you'll be there." He laughed into her expressive, scared eyes. "Oh, come on. What can I get up to with your aunt there? I don't intend to impose on her, if that's what's worrying you. I'll book into a hotel."

"Aunt Leonora is much too hospitable to let you," she said ungraciously in defeat.

She hadn't masterminded her escape campaign very intelligently. Not only had she made a complete hash of it, but the situation was now ten times worse.

Why was he pursuing her in this relentless fashion, stalking her in a manner that was cruel, almost sadistic? Did he think his tenacity would eventually wear her down? Perhaps it would, she thought, going cold with apprehension. He didn't care what lengths he went to. She wasn't taken in. She knew it would take more than Aunt Leonora's presence to put him off. She was weary of fighting. It even crossed her mind that it might be best to give in — let him have his conquest — and then perhaps he'd leave her alone.

Kittiwake Bay had always been a haven to run to when in trouble or pain. One thing was certain: this time Kittiwake Bay would not be the refuge she had come to expect.

Chapter Six

They drove for a while without saying anything, listening in silence to the soothing tones of taped music. When the music finished, however, Noel did not insert another cassette but turned the machine off.

"You're not very talkative," he said.

"Perhaps I haven't anything to talk about. Anyway, you hate small talk."

"True. Tell me about Kittiwake Bay."

"What is there to tell? It's a thriving little village, but it never made it as a seaside resort. A lot of plans were put into operation when the railway came through in the mid-eighteen-hundreds — plots of land were laid out, water mains put in, a reservoir built. The railway was supposed to bring in the day-trippers and holiday-makers from the mill and steel towns. It never caught on as a popular resort, probably because even in summer the conditions are wintry on the exposed moorland heights. They do say it's always attracted more legends than visitors. You've got to be hardy to love it."

"As you do."

"Yes."

She closed her eyes and saw precipitous chalk cliffs massed with ledges and crannies where kittiwakes and other sea birds built their nests; white boulders, swept from places as far away as Scandinavia by past Ice Ages, strewn along the shore like giant meringues, and her own special weakness: fascinating caves just begging to be explored — only at low tide and not by the squeamish.

"Well?" he prompted.

"I cringe to think what you will make of it. It has one hotel, which provides the only bit of nightlife. The town itself 'dies' every evening at six o'clock when everything closes up, right down to the last small snack bar and café. You will find it very dull," she said, with a certain amount of relish.

"On the contrary. It's as though you were describing a piece of heaven. No rush and bustle. Only the clock is wound up — not the people. It placidly ticks out the time of day, and no one is ruled by it. M'm . . . bliss."

She sent him a defensive look. That bland tone was suspect. Was he teasing her? She said tentatively, "There's not much to do except walk."

"Come now, Lorraine. With just a scrap of imagination, I'm sure we can think of something else to do."

She plowed on regardless. "The angels are reputed to go barefoot. You're not an angel —"

"Nor likely to be."

"— so I hope you've had the foresight to pack a strong pair of walking shoes."

"I have."

"There's a path across the clifftop to the abbey ruins, which is one of my favorite picnic spots. If you've got a bit of mountain goat in you, it's fun to scramble down the cliff face and walk all the way along the reef that circles the headland."

"You deplorably uninformed girl, I'll have you know that my birth sign is Capricorn. That's the sign of the goat."

She was not in the least bit surprised. She should have known by his character that he was born under the sun sign ruled by Saturn. He was a typical Capricorn — dark, saturnine, fiercely ambitious, ruthless in his determination to achieve his goal. The type who never gives up.

"If you keep that expression on your face, I shall be reluctant to go anywhere near a clifftop with you. You look as if you're plotting to push me over the edge."

"You wouldn't be the first to go that way, if legend is to be believed. So don't test your luck; history just might repeat itself," she said with an involuntary shiver.

It wouldn't make any difference. The stalwart goat can't be pushed down permanently. The other sun signs fall behind as the mountain goat climbs determinedly from crag to crag on his uniquely designed hoofs. The goat always wins.

During the remainder of the journey she told him a little more about her aunt. "She works in the library and sits on several local committees. Her appearance somehow doesn't fit the role. You'll see what I mean when you meet her. She's a lovely person, in looks and disposition. I'm not too sure of her age."

"Leave it at interesting," he said gallantly.

"I can't understand why she's never married."

"Perhaps she hasn't met the right man yet," he said in stern rebuke, introducing a thought to her mind that hadn't entered it before — that it was early days yet. Aunt Leonora was, after all, only in her forties, and so it was wrong of her to write her off as spinster material for all time. "I always think confirmed bachelors — and that goes for bachelor girls, too — are that way by circumstance rather than inclination," he continued.

"Do you?" she queried, not without surprise and with a dash of suspicion.

Was he saying that, given the right circumstances, if he met the right girl, he wouldn't regard it as "woman's indulgence at man's expense"? Which was, in her estimation, how he had seemed to view marriage.

She might have received the notion with pleasure had she been anywhere else but in a car, with Aunt Leonora waiting at journey's end. Something had just occurred to her which hadn't struck her before. If it had, she would have sat by Noel's side with much more agitation — but she could have done something about it. She could have asked him to stop at a phone box on the pretext of wanting to let her aunt know that she was bringing a guest, but really to warn her not to say anything about her marriage to Jamie. Too late to phone now — they were practically there. Oh, what a tangled web . . . If she didn't handle this carefully, her deception was going to catch up with her.

When they arrived a short time later, she left Noel to bring in the suitcases and raced on ahead into the cottage. Leonora jumped up from her chair and crossed the room to kiss her niece's cheek in greeting. "Where's the fire?" Self-disgust and dismay stamped itself on her face. "Figure of speech. I must stop saying that. How could I? To you, of all people. You caught me off guard by racing in as though you hadn't a second to spare. I'm so sorry."

"It's all right, Aunt Leonora. I —"

"It should be all right. You ought to have got over that nonsense ages ago. I suppose it was reading about him in the newspaper that brought it all back." The eyes, set above the high cheekbones Lorraine had also inherited from her mother's side of the family, were full of frustrated concern. "You sounded calm enough when I spoke to you over the phone, but I wasn't deceived. I knew you were bound to feel something."

"I don't feel anything about Jamie. That's not what I —"

"Have I jumped to the wrong conclusion? I

121

hope I have. I was positive that Jamie had something to do with your sudden decision to visit."

"Only very indirectly." She wished her aunt would keep silent long enough for her to explain. Noel couldn't be far behind. "I've brought a friend with me and I want you to be sure not to —"

"Flap?" As she again anticipated wrongly, Leonora looked down her delicately turned nose and expressed haughtiness in her spread-eagled fingers.

"Aunt Leonora, please *listen* to me."

"Of course I will, dear. When you've satisfied my curiosity on this point. Your friend, is it anyone I know . . ." The words trailed off and her glance was now directed beyond Lorraine's shoulder. The smile in her voice dimpled her cheeks. "You don't have to answer that. I can see for myself it isn't. I'm wondering why." Speculation narrowed her eyes without touching the warmth of her greeting as she said to Noel, "I mean, why don't I know about you?"

With a sinking heart, Lorraine set about remedying that omission. "Aunt Leonora, this is Noel Britton. Noel, my aunt, Leonora Craig."

Leonora was charmed by Noel. From the first compliment he saw to that. "I see now where Lorraine gets her good looks." He went on to comment on the prettiness and delightful location of the cottage, although cottage was something of a misnomer. Leonora's spacious home was low and rambling, with rooms on several different levels.

On the tour of inspection both Lorraine and her aunt found themselves continually warning, "Mind your head!" Or, "Watch that step!"

"I'm afraid these ceilings weren't built to accommodate someone of your height," Leonora informed Noel as they sat in the blue and white parlor drinking tea and eating scones. "To keep you from starving until I can get a meal ready," as Leonora said.

At first Lorraine was on edge, controlling her qualms with difficulty, but gradually her anxiety lessened and she wondered why she had thought it inevitable that her aunt would blurt out some reference to Jamie. Was it because she was used to everything always going wrong? Or was it because she felt guilty at withholding the truth from Noel? It was no use — she didn't want to tell him, but she would have to. If only it could be later. Back home. She didn't want to do anything to spoil her aunt's pleasure at having them there, and she didn't know what Noel's reaction would be when she told him.

And Noel — what had got into him? He was a different man. Going out of his way to be pleasant, displaying a sunny side to his nature that she'd never seen before. She had never guessed he could be like this, and her heart twisted with pride.

In a whispered aside, which he must have heard despite his deadpan expression, her aunt said, "He's a humdinger, Lorraine." She was forced to agree, but not without a small re-pining sigh. Why hadn't he shown himself in this praiseworthy light in Sir William's company?

Noel was most insistent that he could not impose himself as a house guest at such short notice. He said he would be perfectly happy to book a room at the hotel. He had reckoned without Leonora. Most people — and, for all his astuteness, Noel was no exception — were deceived by her gentle expression and slender build. She looked as fragile as the first snow-drop. Perhaps, at that, it was an apt description, because a snowdrop can push its way through even a deep frost. With much the same indomitable determination, she melted Noel's resistance and finally walked out on his noticeably weaker protests to go upstairs to make up the bed in the guest room.

"I see what you mean about her deceptive appearance. Given the choice, I'd rather take on Caesar's invading legions than your aunt. She's a very high-powered little lady."

Lorraine had to smile. "If you're saying that it makes life a whole lot easier to go along with her wishes, I agree. You're not angry at being steam-rollered into staying here, are you?"

"I'm secretly delighted. This beats hotel accommodation any day." Looking relaxed and absurdly comfortable in the fireside wing chair, he announced languorously, "I'm glad I obeyed the impulse to come with you."

She sent him a quizzical look. When it became obvious that she wasn't going to draw anything from him in that oblique way, she tried a more direct approach. "You never actually spelled out why you wanted to come. What motivated the impulse?"

"I spelled it out very precisely. To be with you."

"Flattering, but not the truth."

"Since you know — you tell me."

"I don't *know*, not positively." She gave him a glance from beneath her lashes, and it was fortunate for her peace of mind that she did not know how provocative she looked. "I know you had a bee in your bonnet about Sir William. I don't think you believed that I was coming here to visit Aunt Leonora. You thought I was going off somewhere with him."

His mood altered with a suddenness that was frightening. His jaw tightened, and the bite and derision returned to his tone. "And you think I was so keen to find out — it was so important for me to know — that I would move heaven and earth to alter my plans, rearrange my work schedule at a moment's notice?"

"No," she said, looking chastened as she saw the absurdity of her reasoning.

"There wasn't any reorganizing to do, as a matter of fact," he said bluntly. "I found some unexpected time on my hands with little idea of what to do with it."

She didn't say that she didn't believe him, and the shaking of her head was barely perceptible as she lowered her chin and fixed her eyes on her hands, as though the answer should be there within her grasp. There had to be another explanation. The one Noel had given didn't seem at all like him. Much too indecisive.

She looked up suddenly and found him regarding her with an expression she had detected once or twice before, not taunting or challenging, or even sensual, but — puzzled. As if he found his own actions every bit as mystifying as she did.

Nothing was resolved in her mind, yet an odd feeling of peace was creeping over her, which was a refreshing change from the usual effect his presence had on her. At the same time, she knew that could be changed by a flick of those dark, dominant eyebrows. A look was all that was needed to tauten her nerves and make her cringe from him in fear of giving away the state of her treacherous heart.

"I suppose I should go up and give Aunt Leonora a hand," she said, but she spoke reluctantly and not as though seeking a means of escape. She had tried running away, and that hadn't worked. For some reason, perhaps it was nothing more than feminine perversity, she didn't want to drag herself away from him at this moment when they were alone. And yet, to be alone with him was to want his arms about her.

Which of them planted the idea in the other's mind? Did he, by that strange power he had over her that allowed him to dominate her thoughts, put the fancy there? Or did he read it on her face and respond to it? No matter. He leaped out of his chair, and she was where she wanted to be.

If she was the instigator of this, how foolish it was of her. It was so good to be in his arms, to let her lips respond with fervor to the fierce possession of his mouth; but even as the flame of passion reached an all-time high, her heart dropped in swift dismay.

With her aunt upstairs and the possibility of her bursting in on them at any second prevalent on both their minds, she could enjoy this daring moment, safe in the knowledge that he could not take advantage of her willingness to yield to him. The danger, as the frightened swoop of her heart had been quick to recognize, was in the reckoning that would surely come. Now she could draw back, but later, when time and place were on his side, he would see to it that she didn't back out of the promise she unwittingly kept making.

Suddenly his arms dropped away and she was free. His fingers somewhat awkwardly attempted to smooth her hair. Suspecting that he had heard something she hadn't, she listened. Sure enough, her aunt's footsteps sounded as she descended the stairs.

"That's a remarkably heavy step for such a

dainty female. Most obliging of her," he observed, gaining speedy self-composure. Much to her chagrin, her pulse was still fluctuating wildly and her emotions were tied in knots.

As a further tactful touch, her aunt rattled the doorknob before entering. "You're free to go upstairs now, Noel, if you wish. Your room's all ready. I thought you might like to go up and unpack and perhaps freshen up before dinner."

"Surely," he replied, the easy charm he seemed to have reserved exclusively for her aunt back in place.

Before she could say, "I'll unpack later," seeing this as her chance to have a word with her aunt while Noel was out of the way, Leonora forestalled her. "You can give me a hand with the meal, Lorraine, and do your unpacking later."

It was soon apparent to Lorraine that her aunt had not anticipated her need but had words of her own to air. Following her into the kitchen, and asking what she could do to help, she was surprised to hear Leonora say, "Everything's done. We always have such a lot to talk about when you first arrive that I didn't want to waste my time cooking, so I opted for an easy casserole, something that wouldn't spoil if you were held up. It's simmering away in the oven. I've got a melon to start with, which is sitting in the fridge, and that good old standby, cheese and biscuits, for dessert, so don't have any worries on that score. Now, I want to know all about Noel. I'll start you off by saying that now I've seen him I know you have another reason, apart from lack of avarice, for wanting nothing from Jamie except your freedom."

"Aunt Leonora, the second most important thing you need to know about Noel is that he's the head of the recording company that's got Jamie under contract."

"I get the impression that there's something about the situation that is not as it should be. Perhaps you'd better tell me the most important thing I need to know about Noel."

"He doesn't know I'm married. He doesn't even know that I know Jamie."

"Isn't that rather foolish of you? Honestly, Lorraine, I don't know what I'm going to do with you. You've nothing to be ashamed of, except perhaps not recognizing the weakness of Jamie Gray's character. You should tell Noel. If he's serious about you, it's his business to know. You could find yourself in a very complicated situation."

"I already have, Aunt Leonora. I never meant it to happen like this. I knew I was out of my depth with Noel. Yet I needed someone like him, a cut above the ordinary, to give me back my confidence after the knock I received from Jamie."

"Something I haven't been able to give you, even though I've been telling you for over twelve months now that you look just as good as before."

"Don't be hurt. You are my dear, kind, caring aunt. You're biased. A man took my confidence away; a man had to give it back to me. If that man happened to have a reputation where women are concerned, so much the better. Noel can have his pick. That makes me special. How terribly vain I sound, but I can't help it."

"Oh, my love," despaired Leonora, looking at her niece through eyes that were suddenly brighter than normal. "After all you've been through — the way you looked — the pain you endured so bravely, my darling, during the mending, healing process, with hardly a moan or a protest passing your lips. You've earned the right to be vain. Sir William warned me that the worst scars weren't physical, that the mental scars would take longer to erase. He's been proved right, damn him, but at the time I didn't think he knew what he was talking about. I do know that when I first saw you in the hospital, I came home and wept."

"Jamie wept in front of me. He said I was —" She hid her face in her hands. "I can't repeat it, but he said things I thought would live forever in my mind. If he loved me, he wouldn't have seen me as a freak when I was hurt. If he really loved me, surely the accident would have made him love me even more."

"What you are saying is that Jamie never loved you. His feelings were shallow and never rose above a purely physical level. When you stopped being desirable in his eyes, he left you.

You must know that you were well rid of him."

"I do, yes. But he left me with a terrible bitterness inside. I got it into my head that no man would ever want me in that way again. When Noel made it obvious that he did, I was part way to being cured. I shall always be grateful to him for that." She didn't add, "whatever happens," but the implication rested in the air.

It was this which her aunt replied to. "In this life, relationships don't come with written guarantees. Sometimes you've got to take a chance." Was there a pensive note in her tone, as if she'd missed hers? She seemed to give herself a mental shake, and then said with more briskness, "What's the real problem, Lorraine?"

"I went in with my eyes open. From the beginning I knew that Noel wanted to seduce me. And, if I'm honest, that was part of the attraction for me. After Jamie, it was what my ego needed. I won't blame Noel; you see, I think perhaps I brought it upon myself. I wasn't aware of it at the time, but I played it that way. Subconsciously, I wanted it to be an obsession with him, so that when I'd driven him half crazy with longing I could revenge myself by doing what Jamie had done to me. Walk away. If that was my intention, it's bounced back on me. I've done something very silly. Against all the rules, I've fallen in love with him."

"Oh, *that*," Leonora said on a careless laugh. "You don't have to tell me that. I can see it on your face every time you look at him."

"I hope you can't. That would make me much too vulnerable, because he doesn't love me. Nothing's altered for him. What do I do now? I'm finding it impossible to walk away from him. And when I do, he follows me," she said with a tiny grimace of a smile. "But if I don't make the break . . ." She shook her head to emphasize the point. "No one in her right senses wants to gratify that kind of obsession. I simply don't know how much longer I can hold out against him. Oh, darling Aunt Leonora, I hope I haven't shocked you."

"What do you think I'm made of? I'm not going to wilt at a touch of realism." The tears that had been quick to come to her eyes in compassion were just as speedily glazed over with laughter. "You are extremely conceited if you think your generation invented permissiveness. Which generation gave yours the name tag, do you think? Could they do that without knowing what it's all about? My grandmother — your great-great-grandmother — used to say there was nothing new under the sun. It had all happened to someone at sometime before. And she was right, bless her. I remember another of her sayings. It went something like this: 'Men have always had to be chased to the altar, but the girls who got them there weren't always chaste.' "

"I don't know about that," Lorraine laughed.

"Good," her aunt said. "A smile at last. Seriously, though, Noel is made of sterner stuff than Jamie. I can see he wouldn't be an easy man to have a relationship with. I'd prefer to have him as a friend than a lover."

That remark startled Lorraine. She hadn't believed her aunt to be so perceptive. She had been convinced that the friendliness of the chatter between Noel and her aunt had hidden the electric tension he radiated whenever Lorraine was near.

But when she said as much her aunt merely laughed. "Shock waves fly across the room between you. My goodness, if you can stand the pace, you'll have a terrific partnership. A man like Noel could lead you into ecstasy."

"Yes, but where would that leave me, when he eventually did?"

"You can't be sure he would ever want to leave you." Leonora touched her brow in despair, a gesture that softened the sting of her rebuke. "You never used to be such a pessimist. Jamie's doing again, I suppose."

"I am trying to be realistic. I came into Noel's life at a time when he was bored with insincerity and that streak of hardness underlying the affectations of the women with whom he associated. He sees me as sweetness and innocence — but what's that? Nothing more than a bloom that wears off, and when it does, when his interest cools as it well might, my heartache will be all the greater for having experienced the bliss."

"I can't, in all honesty, advise you. I have no sizzling experience in my past to draw upon, more's the pity. But I still think you've got Noel wrong."

"You mean that's what you hope," Lorraine corrected her. "You haven't known him long enough to form an opinion."

"True, but —" Leonora shrugged her shoulders. "Suddenly I don't feel as worried about you, so explain that. Come on, time to stop discussing the brute and feed him."

"There have been times when I've felt like feeding him to the lions," Lorraine replied wryly. "Aunt Leonora?"

"Yes, my pet?"

"Don't land me in the soup, will you? Don't let anything slip about Jamie."

"I'll be on my guard. But don't be silly about this, will you, Lorraine? You should tell him about your marriage. And soon. The longer you leave it, the harder it's going to be."

"I know. I'll tell him as soon as we get back home. And that's not procrastinating; it's just that I don't want to provoke an awkward situation while we're here. It wouldn't be fair to you, and, anyway, he needs this holiday."

"You're surely not suggesting that he'd storm off and return home?"

"I don't exactly think that. I think he'll want to hear Jamie's side of it. And Jamie has a very plausible tongue." Was she afraid to tell him? Was that the reason for her hesitancy? Did she think that because she hadn't been open with him from the beginning, it would go against her? Would he think she'd been reluctant to speak up because she had something to hide, and would that influence him to take Jamie's part?

"I suppose, having waited until now, it will keep for another week, but don't be afraid of anything that smooth-tongued hypocrite of a husband of yours might say. In other words, don't underestimate Noel, and don't take him for a fool. Does that help any?"

"Thank you, it does."

Leonora's casserole was consumed with great appreciation and received high praise. While they were eating, Lorraine suddenly bethought herself to ask, "Aunt Leonora, I know I didn't give you much warning, but did you manage to arrange time off from work?"

"Yes, I did. But that was before I knew that Noel was coming with you. Not that the time will be wasted. I can find plenty to do in the cottage, so you two can go gadding off with a clear conscience."

"What about your conscience, Leonora? Could you be so cruel?" Noel paused. "You said you were a family who didn't stand on ceremony, so I'm presuming that it's all right to call you by your first name?"

"Thank you, I'd be most grateful if you would. When someone says Miss Craig I feel like taking a peep over my shoulder to see where she is. But — cruel? I thought — tactful."

"I'd much rather take out two pretty ladies than one. So it's definitely cruel to deny me the pleasure of your company."

"The tact is yours, Noel. And there I was, being so self-sacrificing. Sorry, Lorraine, I tried. If I were you I'd want him all to myself and I'd scratch the eyes out of any female who offered to horn in, but I simply cannot resist that charmingly put invitation to join you at least some of the time. He's exclusively yours for the morning exercises if he's crazy enough to join you."

"The operative word being crazy, I take it?" Noel said with an intrigued lift of one brow. "Exercises? Explanation, please."

Leonora supplied it with laughter in her voice. "This ridiculous child gets up practically at dawn and goes galloping over the moors and scrambling along the clifftop and generally seeking out and renewing her acquaintance with all her old haunts. Basic close-to-nature stuff, although I can't see anything natural in it. I told you it was crazy. I leave her to her madness and rise at a more civilized hour."

Next morning, tiptoeing softly so as not to waken a sleeping house, Lorraine sniffed as she approached the kitchen. The rich aroma of coffee was joined by a crackling noise and the equally distinctive smell of bacon being fried.

Looking up from the stove, Noel said, "Your aunt said I should make myself at home, and that's what I'm doing. How do you like your bacon?"

"*After* I've taken my morning walk, when I've worked up an appetite."

"Really? What's wrong with before *and* after? It's my theory that the first breakfast provides the sustenance to find the energy to go out and work up an appetite for the second breakfast." He cut deeply into a loaf of bread, then took two rashers of bacon from the frying pan and transferred them to the two slices of wholemeal bread. "Here you are. No arguments."

"You're too bossy," she said. "I can see I shall have to get my Aunt Leonora to take you down a peg for me." But she accepted the offering, a mouthwatering combination that was heftier than any sandwich she would have prepared for herself.

Taking a giant bite, she wondered why she'd assumed he wouldn't want to accompany her on her more strenuous jaunts. If his splendid physique was anything to go by, he would be able to out-scramble, out-climb, out-race, out-anything her. She ought to have realized that he practiced some regular form of exercise to keep in such good shape. His firm, powerful body was the antithesis of what one might expect in a successful executive. Desk men could often be identified by their paunches and their unhealthy complexions. In his chunky sweater, which complemented the width of his shoulders, and jeans that molded to his lean waistline, slim hips and long, muscled legs, he looked — and her scrutinizing eye speeded the message to her brain on electric waves of awareness — quite undeniably superb.

She brought her eyes back up to his face and was dismayed to see the way his mouth was curling up at the corners, as if he knew she was eating up the sight of him with as much gusto as she was eating her sandwich. Negligible blessing that it was, because his eyes scorched her, he brought his own plate and mug of coffee to the table without comment.

They walked along the clifftop, and because she was familiar with every part of the crumbling coastline, she knew when it was reasonably safe to walk close to the edge and when to keep a healthy distance.

"It's like a scene from a childhood holiday," he observed unexpectedly. "Except that then the sea was blue, not slate gray, and the morning didn't have such a bite and you didn't catch your breath from the cold of it."

"Your holidays were obviously spent on a kinder part of the coast."

"No. Same coastline, further down, that's all. Robin Hood's Bay was a favorite spot. I'm not saying it was *like* that, only that I remember it as being like that."

"Oh, I see," she said, going along with his

nostalgic mood and taking some license of her own when she added, "And there would be no buffeting wind to whip up the sea and toss the gulls around as though they were scraps of paper. Right?"

"Wrong. There was always a good kite-flying wind."

Her mind's eye painted a picture, and she ached because she hadn't known him when he was a volatile boy racing with the wind, poised on the edge of manhood. He had met the challenges that make or break a man and had grown strong with the years. It was inevitable, because nostalgia is catching, that her thoughts should drift back to her own childhood. The endless waiting, the anticipation, then the glorious conclusion of the school term would be upon her, marked by the ending of exams and a languorous leniency stealing over the teaching staff. The sadness at leaving a best friend or special boy, and then off to Kittiwake at last for the long summer vacation. Bracing and breezy, rarely warm enough to lie on the beach in a bikini unless you knew where to find the sheltered suntraps, but somehow a blue and gold summer when touched by memory's alchemy.

They left behind their separate memories and his arms came out and he drew her into a shared memory-in-the-making. The wild roar of the sea and the plaintive mew of the gulls in her ears, his mouth tasting of the salty sea-air cherishing hers in a kiss of sweetness and passion. This would be a memory moment to take out and polish lovingly in the less happy times that were to follow. She knew, with a chill insight that was unexplainable, that pain and heartache were in store for her.

She shivered, and he said quickly, "You're cold. Let's have done with this doddering pace. We'll turn the clock back twenty years and run down to the sea like irresponsible children."

"If the clock were turned back twenty years, that would make me three years old. My legs would be tired and you'd have to carry me."

"What a delicious idea," he said. He clasped an arm around her waist, secured the other under her legs, swept her feet off the ground and started the downhill journey.

She was too frightened to wriggle out of his clasp because of the rocky, steep and dangerously inadequate path. The slightest movement on her part would have them both crashing down, with little hope of finding a sympathetic landing.

Her fears proved to be unfounded. He was as sure-footed as he had claimed to be and deposited her on the beach without mishap and only a little out of breath.

"What do you do for an encore?" she inadvisedly asked, and mentally backed away at the look on his face. "Oh — no." The laughter died on her lips. She couldn't back away physically because, although he had set her feet down on the sand, his arms were still anchored around her.

Two jutting slabs of rock gave them complete privacy. The world was reduced to a narrow spit of sand, a triangle of slate-gray sky flecked with countless mewing kittiwakes, the immensity of the sea and the two of them.

His hands pushed their way under her thick-knit sweater, slid along the smoothness of her back and moved around to the front. So adeptly was it accomplished that she wasn't aware that the slight dalliance in the vicinity of her spine was to unfasten her bra until his fingers came in contact with the bare flesh of her breasts. He stroked and smoothed and molded and held her on points of pleasure; his fingers applied just enough pressure to send her thoughts into a heightened state of exquisite delirium, enough gentleness to make her heart sing at his caring and solicitude.

When he muttered hoarsely, "Oh, God, I want you," the craving was mutual. "It would be idyllic here," he said, his voice a soft groan, a whisper of persuasion across her hot cheek. "Sheltered and peaceful. I can think of no other spot on earth that is so close to nature. You are so beautiful — so desirable. You're driving me insane."

She could feel his urgency in the thickening of his speech, the harshness of his breathing. Even as she shared his torture she put up a hand to push him away, but, instead, her fingers stroked sensuously down his cheek, touching the working nerve at the corner of his mouth.

What had come over her? She could not blame him if he took this gesture as a sign of her willingness, a signal that she would put up no resistance to the natural progression that would take them from the lighter preliminaries of love-play into the searing no-turning-back depths that had but one inevitable outcome.

She couldn't believe it when he was the one to call a halt. It was such an anticlimax to find herself suddenly released that for a moment she almost gave way to hysterical laughter. Her wildly disbelieving eyes raced up to his for explanation.

If anything, the torture was more intense than before. One dark eyebrow lifted in sardonic comment and dark resignation. "It seems that you are to be protected for a while longer by my strong sense of propriety. It might not be your aunt's house, but I am her house guest. It would be like breaking a trust."

In the absurd moment before she regained her senses she found herself wishing that he wasn't such a gentleman. In all her wildest imaginings she could never have foreseen any situation where she would think it a drawback to have a conscience.

Chapter Seven

They continued to enjoy their early morning walks together, irrespective of the changeable weather, which veered from cold and blustery with rain in the teeth of the wind to perfect summer conditions. On one particularly benevolent golden morning it was difficult to resist the treacherous invitation of the sea. Swimming was dangerous because of the strong tides that swept in both directions around the headland, so they walked as usual.

Noel was not the kind of man to keep his hands by his sides on these occasions, but he guarded against a recurrence of that first morning and passions never again flew out of control.

The rest of the time Leonora's objections were overcome and she accompanied them on the excursions by car. Guided by whim, sometimes they ate out at the local hotel or, more often, farther afield; sometimes they returned to the cottage for their evening meal, buckling down to the chores together in friendly compatibility. Once, Noel locked Lorraine and her aunt out of the kitchen, insisting on cooking the meal without female help. Although his voice was quieter on the subject of washing up,

Lorraine was impressed. She hadn't expected him to be so domesticated or such an expert. The meal merited her aunt's laughing comment that she was going to have difficulty in following it.

On the last full day, they drove down the coast to picturesque Whitby, where for a thousand years fishermen and boatbuilders had chosen to build their houses as close as possible to the water's edge.

They parked the car and sauntered along the bustling harbor at a pace that was out of tune with the industry of the fishermen, rugged, leather-skinned types who sucked on their pipes and exchanged seamen's yarns as they worked on their boats, repairing the ravages of one trip in preparation for the next. It was fascinating to watch, and they dragged themselves away with extreme reluctance.

The strong link with the sea was inescapable. They found constant reminders of Captain Cook, who spent the first years of his seagoing career sailing colliers from the port, and of Captain William Scoresby, perhaps a lesser known figure but commemorated with as much enthusiasm for his invention of the crow's nest.

A bangle made of Whitby jet caught Leonora's eyes, and Noel promptly went into the bow-windowed shop and bought it for her.

In thanking him, she said, "I always think it's a great pity that jet lost its popularity because of its association with mourning. It's ironic, re-

144

ally, because if Queen Victoria hadn't taken to wearing it after the death of Prince Albert it might never have been so highly popularized in the first place."

"I hope you share Leonora's liking for jet," Noel said, turning to Lorraine. "I thought you might like these."

The tissue-paper wrapping parted to reveal the wink of black jet in the sensuous shape of long dangling earrings.

"They're lovely," she said with a gasp of delight.

"On you they will be. Ostentatious earrings should only be worn by girls with exceptionally pretty ears."

His eyes laughed darkly into hers, causing fluttering sensations to erupt in her stomach. It was the kind of look he'd avoided giving her during the past week, a deprivation that had not been entirely to her liking even though it had meant she could relax in the company of an extremely entertaining male without holding her breath in constant awareness of his overpowering masculinity.

Although it had been a treat not to be in constant battle with her jangled emotions, the respite had been in no way relaxing. It had crossed her mind to wonder if he no longer found her desirable. She had been divided between pique at his marvelous restraint and dread that he wasn't practicing self-control at all, but that her earlier fears had come true and he had already lost interest in her.

"Put them on," Leonora instructed, pointing to the earrings.

"But they'll look ludicrous with my sweater and jeans," she protested.

"Yes," Leonora agreed. "Put them on."

"Very well."

At lunchtime they turned their backs on the large hotels for the atmosphere of a fish and chip meal at a tiny harbor restaurant. Afterward, they walked back to the car and drove further down the coast to Scarborough, that queen of resorts with its twelfth-century castle perched on the clifftop high above the sea. They ate tricolored ice creams and climbed the steep road leading to the town and its excellent shopping center.

Men normally hate browsing in shops, and the fact that they were there by Noel's guiding hand was highly suspicious. When he disappeared for an hour on an errand of his own, Lorraine was pretty certain that he'd gone to buy her aunt a house gift, although he had more than recompensed her aunt's hospitality by taking them out for meals. When they met up again he wasn't carrying a parcel, but that didn't mean much. It could have been something small enough to slip into his pocket, or he could have returned to the car, which was parked near at hand, and stowed it away in the trunk.

This last supposition proved to be correct.

When they returned to the cottage, Leonora followed her usual custom of going on ahead to open the door and Noel went around to the trunk of his car. Lorraine hovered in curiosity and saw him take out what appeared to be two parcels.

"Well?" she said impatiently when he made no comment. "Aren't you going to tell me what you bought for Aunt Leonora?"

"Will you come up to my room?"

"Noel!"

"Unfortunately, that's not what I have in mind. Good grief, girl! Hasn't my behavior this week proved anything to you? Perhaps you're right," he said, answering the suspicion adhering to her mouth. "I've taken more cold showers in the last seven days than cleanliness warrants. Your guess that I absented myself to buy my hostess a parting gift was right on target. You know Leonora's taste better than I do. I wanted to ask your opinion. So, will you come up to my room?" His eyes were in conflict with his words. They said, "Dare you?"

She answered his eyes. "You wouldn't . . . would you?"

"Only one way to find out," he taunted.

He wasn't being very gallant to tease her like this. He was paying her back for not being more trusting. She couldn't deny him that right. But how far did he intend to go in retaliation? Words she could handle. To quote the ones he'd just used, "Only one way to find out."

She walked ahead of him with dignity in her step. He followed her into the bedroom. That was a mistake. She should have let him go first to claim the option of leaving the door open. He closed it behind him.

He put the parcels he had been carrying down on the bedside table and took a long slender box from his pocket. He opened it and lifted out a bracelet. It wasn't until he fastened it around her wrist that she realized it wasn't an inexpensive piece of costume jewelry, like the jet earrings. It was the prettiest bracelet she had ever seen, delicately designed in twists and circles of gold, and some of the circles contained the sparkle of diamonds.

"You've gone overboard with the price. It's much too costly and too personal for Aunt Leonora to be able to accept it."

"It wasn't intended for Leonora." He indicated the parcels he had just put down. "Leonora's present is there. I bought the bracelet for you."

"That's even worse. I can't accept jewelry from you."

"You accepted these," he said, touching the swing of jet at her ears.

"That's different and you know it. A token. Here, you must take it back."

"I'm sorry if I've offended you," he said stiffly, his voice as cold as hers had been heated, taking the bracelet and tossing it carelessly down on the bed, making her cringe involuntarily at the ill-treatment of such an exquisite thing. "This is what I bought for Leonora. I was torn between a piece of glass and this —" Discarding the outer wrapping, he opened a box, and from her protective straw bed he lifted a porcelain ballerina, perfect in pose and detail.

"It's beautiful," she said, taking it reverently in her hands. "It's still too costly and Aunt Leonora will scold you for going to such expense, but it's in good taste and she will love it."

"I get the message. Giving you the bracelet wasn't in good taste. It didn't say the right thing. Apparently, that's as important as the cost of the item." He unwrapped the other box and took something from it. "While I was in the shop, this little chap caught my eye. Does he say the right thing to you?"

This time she accepted the gift, a china cupid, into her careful fingers. "He's adorable," she said. He was smaller than the ballerina, about a quarter of the size, but he bore the same very exclusive maker's stamp. "I shouldn't, really. But yes, thank you," she said, reaching up to kiss him.

He cupped her face in his hands, tenderly protective of the china cupid still within the clasp of her fingers. Her mouth received his kiss, but there wasn't a part of her mind or body that didn't react to the ecstasy of it. He kissed her again, releasing a second wave of passion within her, and her lips turned to fire. She knew it was time to go, only her feet wouldn't act of their own volition. She needed a push.

He supplied it. "For pity's sake, Lorraine! I'm not made of steel. That bed is too available and too inviting, and so are you. If you don't get out of here quickly —"

She didn't wait for him to finish the sentence.

Somewhere outside a blackbird was singing its heart out and the sun skipped in at her window and laid its warm finger on her eyelids, tempting her lashes open. The china cupid, which she hadn't dared to refuse after annoying Noel by not accepting the bracelet, sat on her dressing table — her dressing table at home and not Aunt Leonora's dressing table at the cottage — where she could see him instantly on waking.

Her smile was as full of joy as the blackbird's song as she said to the cupid, "When he gave you to me, do you suppose he was trying to tell me something?"

But when the days that followed brought no word from Noel, she began to wonder if she'd perhaps read too much into the gift. Every time she was called to the phone her heart lifted, then dropped when it wasn't him.

When he did eventually phone her, his voice was terse and preoccupied.

"Lorraine, I've got a crisis on my hands. I

haven't time to explain now. I've sent a taxi to collect you and bring you to my apartment. Don't argue. Get in it and come."

Such arrogance was typical of him. He left her hanging around for days on end, and then snapped his fingers and expected her to come running.

Now that they were on home ground, had he reverted to type? Was the urgent request a trick to get her into his apartment? It was a risk she would have to take. She had made up her mind that the very next time they met she would tell him about her marriage to Jamie. Noel's apartment would supply the privacy she needed.

She hadn't tried to get in touch with Jamie to ask for her freedom because she knew that he was still in America. Yesterday's late edition had carried a news story about him, a report of his being involved in a nightclub fracas. Noel would be furious about that. She knew that it was not unusual for such publicity stunts to be arranged just to attract attention and bring in the customers. Noel didn't operate that way. He was conscious that a proportion of the public consisted of teen-agers, and he wouldn't deliberately promote anything he saw as a bad influence. Jamie's entire publicity campaign had been built round his clean-cut image. With his childish blue eyes and his golden hair, Noel had been quick to see that Jamie was tailor-made for the part of boy charmer. He was the answered prayer of every mother who feared for the hazards that lay in wait to beset her naive and impetuous young daughter.

It was in the cards that sooner or later Jamie would do something to discredit himself, but why did he have to do it just now? Noel would be seething as it was without her adding her piece. Yet putting it off again could serve no useful purpose. Might as well pile on the infamy while Jamie was well out of reach of Noel's anger.

She didn't know how Noel would react when she told him everything — it would depend on the depth of his affection for her — but it could only be to Jamie's advantage if he was not around until the first shock had worn off.

The taxi arrived before she had time to change and freshen up. The urgency of his phone call must have got through to her because she turned on her heel, unwilling to keep the driver waiting. He dropped her off at a very exclusive apartment block and waved aside her attempt to pay, assuring her that it would be charged to Mr. Britton's account.

She walked into the building, and it was like entering another world, a plush, sumptuous world she had seen only on film and had thought to be wildly exaggerated because no one could live in such luxury.

A man came hurrying toward her, an ingratiating smile on his lips. "Miss Marshall?"

She nodded to indicate her identity. She was trying to look as though it was commonplace for her to receive VIP treatment and this could only be achieved by keeping her mouth closed. Her voice at that moment would have revealed the truth.

He guided her toward the elevator, where the doors were open and waiting to transport her straight up to the penthouse suite. It was like walking in a dream. She had known that he was not short of money, yet nothing about him had hinted that he could afford to live in this style of unpretentious good taste and comfort put before fashion, which found favor in her eyes.

The open door invited her to enter the lounge where soft, melodious music was coming from the stereo, but there was no sign of Noel. From the other side of another open door, his unmistakable voice called out, "I'm in here. Come in and make yourself useful."

It could have been the kitchen and he might have been inveigling her into fixing him a snack. But it was his bedroom. An open suitcase sat on his king-sized bed and he was throwing clothes into it. This fact made it less of a shock to see that he was wearing a blue silk robe, little more than thigh level, with no apparent evidence of anything underneath. She noticed three things. His chest was muscular and very hairy. His legs, their length emphasized by the shortness of his robe, were strong and deeply tanned. And his hair was wet from the shower he had obviously just taken.

He noticed one thing about her: the blush

staining her very expressive face. "Hello, darling," he said, pausing in his task to drop a kiss on her cheek before commenting on the obvious cause of its heightened color. "Does this bother you?" Indicating his robe.

She supposed it was respectable coverage at that, and she felt that it was very gauche of her to be so completely mesmerized by the sight of him and so compellingly conscious of the male aura he emitted in this state of undress. "Well," she bluffed in embarrassment.

"It never fails to get me," he said.

"What?"

"That blush. I won't be a moment." He disappeared into the bathroom. When he reappeared he was still wearing the robe and its deep wrapover vee fastening still exposed his hairy chest, but now his legs were correctly encased in trousers. He looked down at her from his great height and his strained face softened in tolerance. "I'm a lucky guy to have found you first. I was beginning to think that a man had to catch a girl before her sixteenth birthday to say that."

"Noel, there's something I should —"

"Let me finish. This is going to be a flowery speech, and that's something I haven't a lot of experience to draw on. The world I knock around in is corrupted by avarice and self-gratification, where girls not only grab diamond bracelets but demand the matching necklace as well, so you must excuse me for thinking you

154

couldn't be true. Well, it's taken time, but now I know you are."

"Noel, I must tell you —"

"Later. Please listen. I've wanted you from the first moment I saw you. Every move I made was to one end: to get you between the sheets. My feelings on that score haven't lessened; in fact, they're getting more urgent and intense by the moment. I don't know how long I can go on putting your virtue before my carnal desire. I can see only one way that will satisfy us both, and that's to make it legal. Think about it and have your answer ready for me when I come back, bearing in mind that I will only accept a yes."

"Oh, *Noel*."

"Don't look at me like that. Help me to finish my packing, or so help me I'll kick the suitcase aside, say to hell with Jamie Gray, take what your eyes are offering and see about the legal aspect later."

She was almost swooning with happiness. Noel had just . . . proposed? Somehow, miraculously, he had found out about Jamie, he didn't mind and he was going to sort it out with him. She didn't have to do a thing, just sit back and wait until it was all taken care of.

But no — she went over his words again in her mind and realized that something didn't fit. He hadn't spoken as if he knew of her marriage to Jamie. She shook her head, trying to rid herself of confusion, and remembered Noel's own connection with Jamie, who was in Las Vegas, and, if one could believe what one read in the press, was getting himself into a whole lot of trouble. That's what Noel would be going to sort out.

"You don't mind if I finish my packing while we talk, do you?" he said. "Planes won't wait and I haven't a lot of time."

"It must be something very important to make you fly out to see him."

"It is. He's been acting the fool. You may have read about it in the papers — arriving late for performances, turning up drunk out of his mind, gambling excessively. Finally he got himself involved in a fight that ended up with someone almost getting killed. I've sent cables, which he hasn't answered. I've tried to reach him by phone. I'm now going out there to deliver an ultimatum. He can pull himself together or I'm going to sue for breach of contract. That's if I don't give him grounds to sue me first by taking it out of his hide."

"You sound very angry," she said in understatement.

"With complete justification. Time and money have been invested in promoting his image — but this can't be of interest to you." He pushed the last few things into his suitcase, closed the lid and slammed home the locks. "We have so little time before I have to dash for my plane."

He didn't know about her and Jamie. Her

happiness of a moment before was suddenly dashed to pieces.

"Darling —" His arms came strongly round her. "Don't be so desolate. I'll only be gone a few days and then —"

She knew that his mind was desperately divided. He didn't want to leave her. He released her with deep reluctance. He threw off his robe and reached for his shirt, buttoned it up and tucked it into his trousers.

There was a tie on his bed which complemented his shirt and had obviously been left out to wear. She held it out to him.

"Thanks. Pass me my jacket, there's a love. You were trying to tell me something." He was looking at the bedside clock. "What was it?"

It wasn't something she could gabble out in a few seconds. And in any case, how could she tell him *now?* She owed Jamie nothing; his own actions had killed any loyalty she might have had, but she could not do it to him. It was one thing to tell Noel of Jamie's treachery with the cooling ocean between them to lower the heat of his temper. But Noel was crossing that ocean to see Jamie, and he was murderous minded enough toward him as it was without her adding fire to his fury.

He took her into his arms, and there was pain in his eyes at the enforced parting. His lips moved over her forehead and down her cheek in one long, sliding, blissful kiss that drenched every part of her body in its warmth and blessed her soul.

"Oh . . . my lovely Lorraine." Her name emerged on a husky, wrung-out note, as if he were generating more emotion than he could handle. She willingly, adoringly absorbed it into her own heart, wrapping her arms round his neck in deep, humble, throat-swelling gratitude.

He lusted for her. That hadn't changed. The heat of his desire scorched down her body, and she wouldn't have had it any other way. But now she sensed a subtle difference. Always before she had known that higher feelings didn't enter into it and that he had wanted her solely to sate the demands his body was making. Somehow — how? when? — his heart had become involved. If he wasn't in love with her already, he was moving swiftly in that direction.

"It's hell leaving you. You know that, don't you, precious?" he said thickly.

"I know," she murmured.

Compulsively, their mouths leaped together again, and were dragged agonizingly apart.

"What was this all-important thing you had to tell me?"

"Did I make it sound all-important?" She shrugged, smiled and said, with no idea of the disastrous consequences she would bring upon herself, "It will keep until you get back."

Chapter Eight

While Noel was away, one nice thing happened to create a pleasant diversion. Sir William phoned to invite her out to dinner, and she accepted without giving herself time to wonder about the wisdom of this. Noel hadn't liked Sir William because he was jealous of him. Once he knew he had no cause to be jealous there would be no cause for resentment. It was as simple as that.

The preliminaries of greeting out of the way, Sir William said, "Correct me if I'm wrong, but aren't you the girl who likes authentic Greek cooking?"

"I'll correct you. You're wrong. It's Aunt Leonora who is mad about moussaka."

"Pity. I hope that doesn't sound too ungallant; it's just that I know this charming little taverna. Still, no matter. What does set your taste-buds dancing?"

"Sweet and sour. Crispy noodles, giant prawns — oh, and those little pancake rolls."

"Good. I don't mind Chinese myself. By the way . . . how is your charming aunt?"

It was a natural enough enquiry, yet a certain eagerness in his tone alerted her senses to something she had previously been unaware of.

Why hadn't she noticed before the slight embarrassment when he spoke her aunt's name, as if he were guilty of self-betrayal? And, now she came to think of it, there was a similar reaction whenever she mentioned Sir William's name to her aunt. Leonora always went girlishly pink and suddenly became absorbed with her hands. Sir William and Aunt Leonora — what a lovely thought. No aunt was loved more, and Sir William would always hold a special place in her heart.

"My aunt is very well," she replied. "I've recently returned from visiting her." Casting out a speculative line, wondering what reaction it would get, if any, she said, "It's Aunt Leonora's turn to visit me next time."

Not only did he go for the bait, he knew he was going for it. He smiled, crinkling up his eyes at the corners, intensifying their blueness and looking boyishly vulnerable despite his abundance of silver hair. "And I thought I was being very subtle. Keeping it all to myself. Perhaps you should tell me what I'm going to say next."

"Something along the lines of . . . 'when your aunt visits you, give me a ring and I'll book a table for two at that Greek taverna I was telling you about'?"

"Your aunt might not be in favor."

"Oh, but she will. You have my word for it. Remember, she's mad about moussaka."

"I hope you're right, young lady, because it

seems as though I'm going to find out."

She beamed in delight, despite feeling like the sprat out to catch the mackerel.

"Come on," Sir William said with pretend briskness. "All this talk of food is making me hungry. Let's stop talking about it and find it — I've somewhere in mind that I think you will like."

She did like it, approving the quiet efficiency of the staff and the general aura of the place.

Smiling across the table at her, Sir William told her how nice she looked.

She had been undecided about what to wear, and, after an initial hesitation, she had settled for a dress she had purchased only the day before. It was an ideal opportunity to get the male viewpoint before wearing it for Noel. It had about it an elusive quality — some hidden factor responsible for its appeal which she couldn't define. Its coloring had none of the compelling blatancy of the sun, nor the beguiling brilliance of the sunset. It glowed with a more gentle radiance. She was charmingly unaware that she was that elusive quality; the eye-compelling factor that set off its delicate dawn sweetness was herself.

It was gratifying to know that her appearance found approval in Sir William's eye, but it was no longer the morale booster she had so desperately needed before Noel came into her life. His interest had given back to her the confidence which Jamie had stolen.

"Not only do I like the new dress —" Sir William paused. "It is new, isn't it?"

"Yes."

"What color would you say it was?"

"Peach."

"That's very appropriate, because you look a peach in it."

"Thank you, kind sir," she said, smiling radiantly with none of the former doubt and diffidence she had shown when receiving a compliment.

That fact had not escaped Sir William's shrewd eye. "As I was saying, not only do I like the new dress, but I also like the new you. Obviously a man's influence. I hope he's as good to you as he is for you. I suppose it's that fellow you introduced me to when we last met."

She had to laugh at his begrudging tone. He hated it to be Noel who was behind her newfound confidence. "I know you have every right to disapprove of Noel. He went out of his way to antagonize you, but it was only a mood. And, anyway, you wouldn't know him now, he's altered so much. He's kind, considerate and so patient. You wouldn't believe —" She laughed and shook her head in gentle emphasis. "I can hardly believe the difference in him myself. At the risk of sounding immodest, I think I am a good influence on him."

Still looking skeptical, Sir William said, "And has this reformed character proposed marriage yet?"

"In a manner of speaking. But I'm hoping to get a proper proposal when he gets back."

"Gets back?"

"From seeing Jamie."

"Oh, so you've told him about Jamie. I'm so gla—"

"No, I haven't," she inserted quickly.

"But I thought you said — Forgive me, I'm slightly confused."

"I believe I mentioned that they had a business connection. Noel's company has got Jamie under contract. Jamie got a very good booking in Las Vegas, where he is now. It seems that he's been acting the fool, attracting the wrong kind of publicity, and Noel's gone to straighten him out. I would have told Noel about us — I was on the point of doing so — but then I thought that Jamie would have enough to explain as it was and it would be kinder to save my piece until later."

He looked at her as though he couldn't believe his own ears. "Are you telling me, girl, that after all Jamie has done to you, you're considering him? You're a fool! You should have told your man everything and let him sort it all out in one go. Might have been a kindness, you know, for Jamie to have got it over in a lump rather than in dribs and drabs."

"Yes." She sighed. "That crossed my mind, too."

"What did happen, Lorraine?"

"You mean . . . three years ago? You know what happened."

"No, I don't. Leonora only told me as much as I needed to know. I'd like to hear your version. Unless you'd find it too painful to talk about?"

She shook her head crisply. "It doesn't bother me now. I'm better inside as well as outside. It was ironic, really, but my life, the life I knew, ended when Jamie's took off. I didn't know him very well when he asked me to marry him."

"That, my dear," Sir William interrupted dryly, "was obvious."

Her smile forgave him the dig. "I thought I was in love with him. I wasn't, of course; I was in love with the idea of being in love. And perhaps I was lonely. My father had recently died and I was looking for someone to fill the gap. Aunt Leonora knew that Jamie wasn't the answer. She tried to warn me, but I wouldn't listen. We planned for a quiet wedding — Jamie had no near relatives, so just Aunt Leonora and a few close friends — and then we were going to Cornwall for our honeymoon. The wedding took place, but the honeymoon had to be cancelled. A big-name star fell ill and Jamie was asked to step in at a moment's notice. This was it; the break every artist holds his breath for. So instead of Cornwall we booked into a hotel just around the corner from where he was appearing. I saw the show, but I didn't hang around afterward. He was advised to keep our marriage secret for the time being, in case it spoiled his chances. This opportunity had been too long awaited for him to take any risks. I returned to our hotel, and Jamie was going to join me later. I was dropping on my feet — with one thing and another it had been quite a day — and so I went to bed." She paused and gave a long shuddering sigh.

"You don't have to go on," Sir William said, his keen eyes scrutinizing her expression.

"Don't pander to me. I'm all right. The smell of smoke must have woken me up. I have no way of knowing how long the bed had been smoldering. I think it may well have caught fire as I opened my eyes because I was staring petrified at an orange wall of flames. I got out of bed and somehow found the door and made my way into the corridor — and then I realized that the fire hadn't started by itself. I guessed, and as it turned out my hunch was correct, that Jamie had come back. It seemed probable to assume that he had got into bed with a lighted cigarette, and that that was the cause of the fire. Then it struck me. What if he was still in there?"

"I know the bit that comes next. You fought your way back through the smoke, which was now even denser, and you attempted to beat out the flames and suffered severe burns, mainly to your hands — only to find that Jamie wasn't there."

"He'd had quite a few drinks after the show. After the tension he must have been going through, that was understandable, I suppose."

"You are too understanding. A man who can't take drink — shouldn't. I'm sorry, Lorraine. It's difficult enough for you as it is. You can certainly do without my interruptions."

"According to the forensic report the fire was started by a lighted cigarette. Jamie admitted to lighting a cigarette, but he couldn't remember much else, except wanting to go to the bathroom. The bathroom was along the corridor, and that's where he was. I got burned for nothing. That was the stupidity of it."

"I knew you were on honeymoon, but I didn't realize it was the first day of your honeymoon. And so you are — ? No — that's a gullible assumption to make in this day, and, in any case, it's none of my business and it's a damned impertinence."

"You are quite right; I am a virgin. And it's not an impertinence from you. We hadn't made love before, and we were too busy that day. Straight after the ceremony Jamie was plunged into a hurriedly arranged rehearsal for the night's show. When he came back to the hotel —" She made an expressive gesture with her hands. "I've already explained about that. And so the marriage was never consummated. I once looked up the word consummated in a thesaurus. Among its meanings I read the words 'to crown, to perfect.' In view of Jamie's horror when he came to see me in the hospital, it would have been a crown of thorns. I'm sorry. I'm being melodramatic and I promised myself I wouldn't be."

"And neither are you. I'm impressed that you have your emotions in such marvelous control. You don't have to tell me what happened after that. I was there, remember, a very angry witness to that weakling's despicable behavior. When he hid his face in his hands and blubbered — like the child he proved himself to be — that he couldn't bear to look at you, I knew you were better off without him. My relief at his hasty departure was not untouched by worry. I was afraid of the psychological effect on someone of your sensitivity. I could repair the physical defects — use my skill to repeal the penalty you paid for *his* carelessness; I was not empowered to erase the deeper damage he inflicted upon you by his cowardice. The wrong person paid. You — the innocent party — suffered. He got off scot-free. I still think, as I thought then, that you should seek redress. It's still possible. I will help you." His eyes fixed on her with eagerness glinting in their bright depths. "It's been on my conscience that I let that side, the financial aspect of the situation, drift. You and your aunt were alone. You needed some muscle behind you to protect your rights. I should have supplied it. In that respect I've always felt that I failed you."

"That's absurd. My reply would have been the same then as it is now. I want nothing from Jamie except my freedom."

"That's strange."

"That I've decided I want my freedom?"

"No. That Jamie hasn't asked for his before now. Assuming, of course, that he hasn't approached you about a divorce. In view of what you've just told me, I should say annulment."

"No. Jamie has made no attempt to get in touch with me, personally or through another party."

"Why, do you suppose?"

"It struck me as being odd, too, but I've always thought that he couldn't be bothered."

"Very likely. Something unpleasant and Jamie can be relied upon to avoid it. And now, I'm not going to permit one more word on the subject of that distasteful young idiot. Let's talk of something else and enjoy our meal."

Sooner than she thought — in a matter of days, as he promised, and not the extended period she feared — she received the telephone call she had been waiting for.

"I'm home, darling."

"Noel? Is it you?"

"It had better be, or you'll have to answer for it. No one but me is allowed to call you darling."

"It's just that you — your voice — it sounds

strange. Have you been drinking?"

"Try again."

"Tired?"

"You got it. Come around to my apartment in about four hours, when I've caught up on some sleep. Call a taxi and have it charged to my account. Unless you're going to make me do the courtship bit and come around and get you?"

"I wouldn't be so cruel. Go to bed. I'll join you later."

"M'm. Like the sound of that," he growled wickedly.

"In your apartment."

"What else could I have thought you meant? Frankly, I'm so dead beat you could crawl into bed beside me and I'd still go to sleep."

"You won't mind if I take your word for it? I'd prefer not to put you to the test."

He chuckled. "Wise girl. See you."

She spent the waiting time constructively in taking a shower, washing her hair, selecting something to wear and rejecting it in favor of something else, finally settling for the first choice, the peach dress she had tried out on Sir William.

She ought to tell him about her evening out with Sir William; with her luck someone was bound to have seen them out together and would inform Noel if she didn't. She laughed lightly at the thought of his ridiculous jealousy, thinking it showed a touching lack of vanity.

The knowledge that other men would have difficulty in competing with his strong good looks was readily available. All he had to do was look in his own mirror. Alternatively, he could look into her eyes to know that, after him, all other men were nonstarters.

He was up and about when she arrived at his apartment — if only just. His eyes were less alert than usual, his hair was tousled from sleep. She suspected that but for contacting her he would have slept the clock round. He was wearing the blue silk robe she had found so unnerving, but perhaps he had remembered her previous shyness, for he was wearing trousers underneath.

He pulled her into his arms and rubbed his stubbly chin gently across her cheek. His body, lean but toned to peak perfection, carried weight when it came to male potency. Her joy in him found outlet in the singing of her flesh, the excited awareness of her heartbeat.

To maintain any kind of balance, her senses required constant vigil. His body, warm from sleep, his virility, went to her head. Her slipping senses lost that vital grip and she was no longer in control of the situation. It was controlling her — controlling them both, because the desire-glazed look in his eyes and the drumming beat of his heart's blood told her that he was mindlessly drifting on the natural urges and impulses of his body.

Her longing for him made her dizzy; that he

wanted her as fiercely was evident in the hungry possession of his lips on hers. She was coming up for breath for the third time when she heard him groan, "Hell, no."

He might be stronger minded than she was, but he wasn't finding it easy. He was obviously involved in a desperate struggle to regain command. He managed it, and her yielding body was pushed gently but firmly away. "You showed that you trusted me by coming here."

"Of course." Her eyes were huge. "If I didn't trust you, there would be no point in going on."

His face was dark with passion, and the grip he had on her upper arms corresponded with the tight grip he was having to assert on himself. "I won't betray that trust. When I asked you to come around here, it was unspoken between us that nothing would happen. I won't go back on that. I value your opinion of me too much."

She looked down at her hands. They were trembling. Not because of what would have happened if he hadn't called a halt, but because it hadn't happened. Her own desires unappeased, she was finding it difficult to applaud his high principles.

"Trust is a two-way thing," she said unsteadily.

"So?"

"There's something I must tell you."

"I'm listening."

"While you were away, Sir William phoned me and invited me out for a meal. I could see no harm in it, and so I went. I'm telling you this because I don't want to lose Sir William's friendship because you have got the wrong impression of his interest in me. Also, if I don't tell you, someone else probably will. That's one confession out of the way."

"Which implies you are about to make another." His voice was stiff with objection. He was angry with her for going out with Sir William when she knew that he would disapprove.

But his disapproval was completely without foundation. If he would stop chasing ahead of himself, if he just waited and let events take their natural course, he would see that Sir William's thoughts on that score lay in a different direction. The woman he was attracted to was Leonora, not her niece.

The satisfaction of knowing that time would prove him wrong wasn't going to help her at this precise moment. She'd made a mistake by not plunging straight into the main issue: her marriage to Jamie. She had thought that she could lead into it gently by referring first to Sir William, whose name was inseparably linked with that period of her life. She had been wrong. Noel's dark, saturnine head, sitting on well-muscled shoulders, was held at a belligerent angle that did not augur well for the confession she was about to make. With a sinking heart she knew that he was not going to listen to her in sympathy.

"I suppose that lecherous silver-tongued Lothario wasn't satisfied with fawning over you. And I'll bet he didn't stop at kissing your hand!" Dark eyes under contemptuous brows drilled piercingly into hers, the flash of steel-gray sarcasm disarming and forewarning. "Is that what this second confession is about? Did he get you into bed?"

"No!" Her color rose. "I've told you before. It's not like that between us. He's a fine man and a good friend."

His expressive eyebrow shot up. "You did say he was a man? So if I'm not to question his masculinity, am I to presume that he wouldn't try to get you into bed until he'd put a ring on your finger?"

She shook her head in despair. "You're obsessed with the idea that there's something going on between us, but there isn't. But yes, as you are so insistent, if there were, then Sir William would get his priorities right. He hasn't asked me to marry him because his interest lies elsewhere. And stop implying that I regard my body as an item of barter, something I'm only prepared to give in exchange for a wedding ring. It makes me sound cold and calculating and I'm not."

"You are not cold. I can vouch for that."

"Does that mean I can come down from that pure and untouched pedestal where you put me and where I've never belonged?"

A flicker of something touched his eye, then hardened into sarcasm. "What are you saying, my love? That you're not pure and untouched?"

She was angry now. There seemed to be no way to break it gently to him. She might as well blurt it out and get it over with. "What I'm saying is that I'm married."

Chapter Nine

"Say that again," he demanded.

The look on his face made her quail. "I didn't mean to break it to you as starkly as that, but you goaded me into it." She bit hard on her lower lip. "I'm sorry, Noel. It's true; I am married. I know I should have told you before."

"Too right you should. My God, what a laugh! I've been tying myself in knots not to touch you, and if I'd known from the beginning that you were another man's leftovers I might not have wanted to." His equanimity was frightening. There was a tensile quality about it. Any moment it would snap. "It's so incredible that I'm tempted to say I don't believe you. But why would you lie about such a thing? You've nothing to gain — and much to lose. Why the hell didn't you tell me?"

"Perhaps because deep down I was afraid to. I knew you'd react this way. Whether you like it or not, I had a life before we met. I haven't been preserved in ice waiting for you to find me."

"Where is your —" He swallowed, obviously choking on the word — "husband?"

"He — Jamie — left me."

"Jamie?"

"Jamie Gray."

That was the snapping point. Without a word he seized her by the arms in a powerful grip and shook her until her jaw locked and a swirling whorl of red mist floated before her eyes. "There couldn't be two Jamie Grays. You do mean the one I've been with these past few days? It is *that* Jamie Gray?"

"Yes," she said, wondering at his insistence in making that point clear.

One hand released its cruel hold, but only to transfer itself to her chin, forcing her head back, making her see the contempt expressed on his face. Only then did he speak. "So you're the cause of all this trouble. You are Jamie's scheming little wife."

"I'm married to Jamie, yes. That doesn't give you call to abuse me." The interruption went unheeded. Had she spoken? Or if she had, was the only voice at her command too low for him to hear?

"You've slipped up badly this time. You should have stuck to barter — it would have been more profitable. Dallied me on a while longer and set about getting a nice quiet divorce from Jamie. I was so desperate for your body that I would have considered a wedding ring a fair exchange. But no, you were too greedy. You had to go in for blackmail as well."

"Blackmail? What are you talking about?"

"Don't act the innocent. You've played that role out. Jamie and I have done a lot of talking these past few days. He's told me everything."

"Jamie has?" she inquired hoarsely.

"That's what I said. He told me it was a whirlwind romance and that you went into marriage without really knowing one another, and all the sordid details of how you couldn't stand the penny-pinching struggling days and the inevitable separations while he established himself in his career. And how you only got in touch with him when you realized he'd made it and you decided you wanted a share of the big time."

"It's not true, not all of it. The whirlwind romance bit is true. We did go into marriage without knowing one another. But as for the rest — no!"

He ignored her. She might not have spoken. "I don't blame my secretary for giving you his address. It wouldn't have needed a lot of detective work on your part to find it out for yourself. I wondered how you knew her name that time you waited for me in my suite at the club. 'I thought that was Miss Brown's office,' you said. Bad slip of the tongue that. Incriminating. You're not going to deny contacting my secretary to find out Jamie's whereabouts?"

"No. It's true that I phoned the club and spoke to Miss Brown in the hope of getting Jamie's address. But it was too late. He'd already left for the States."

"That's rich. It was not too late. You saw Jamie before he went. It was the biggest break he's ever likely to get, and you fouled it up for him."

"Me?"

"Yes, you. He blames his current fall from grace on the worry you caused him just when he could least deal with it."

"This is unbelievable. What am I supposed to have done?"

"Threatened to expose him. Don't tell me your memory's that bad. You told him that if he didn't come over handsomely with a slice of the earnings, you intended to give — correction, sell; your sort gives nothing — to the press the intimate and highly personal details of your marriage. It goes without saying that you would add a few unsavory frills of your own for titillation, to command a higher fee."

"It's simply not . . . true," she said, but she was wavering.

"You don't sound very positive. Decided to stop lying?"

"I am not lying. If I sounded unsure for a moment, it's because all this ties in with a recent conversation I had with Sir William. He thinks Jamie should be made to pay. Just for a moment I wondered if he'd approached Jamie without consulting me, but it isn't possible. You say this happened before Jamie went to the States? I didn't meet up with Sir William again until after that, so it couldn't have been him."

"Nice try, but why don't you admit that the game's up? Or —" His eyes flicked over her —

"perhaps it's just starting."

"What do you mean by that?"

"Guess. You were right, you know, I did put you on a pedestal. I worshipped at your feet. Not right at the beginning. I admit that at first I thought you were the same as the rest. Then — you really fooled me. I went for all that virtue and innocence in a big way. You practically emasculated me. I had no inclination to look at another woman. I couldn't tear myself away from that legendary playground, Las Vegas, fast enough to come back to you. I was going to ask you to marry me. Kindly note the tense; I said *was*."

"I know you were. I don't know what's gone wrong. I don't understand any of this. The best thing I can do now is to go home. Later, when we've both reasoned things out, perhaps we can talk about it more coolly."

"You aren't going anywhere." His hold on her arm increased; his eyes flashed their menacing message. "You initiated the game. Go away, come closer, yes, no. You've had my emotions on a swivel. Promising, withdrawing, overtaking me and then slamming on the brakes. You've had your fun. Now I'm going to have mine."

"What — are you going to do?"

"Make your intimate acquaintance. I could put it a coarser way. "

"No!"

The blood drained from her face. She felt

weak and defenseless against his strength as in one fluid, effortless movement he held her against him, her feet treading air, and carried her into his bedroom.

"I've revered you," he said thickly. "Now I'm going to ravish you."

"Please don't, Noel. There's something I mus—" His mouth came down on hers, suppressing the words.

She tried to keep her lips in a tight compressed line to shut him out. But the fierce pressure of his sensual mouth made her gasp with dizziness. He made the most of the opportunity, kissing her as if he could never get enough of her, holding her in total domination so that not one single part of her was immune. The fire on her lips spread through her veins until she thought her body would melt under the intense heat.

"Oh . . . no," she moaned.

His hands deftly changed position and she found herself sliding down the length of his body and stopping, held close, her feet still several inches from the ground. She felt the heat of his angry passion through the thin material of her dress. She slithered the rest of the way until her feet touched the ground. He was in too much of a rage to undress her in a civilized fashion. Her beautiful peach dress was ripped from her shoulders, leaving her breasts exposed in dainty cups of peach satin and lace. Her arms were imprisoned so that she couldn't put up even a token resistance to beat him off.

"No," she moaned again, but her plea fell on deaf ears. She still had two legs to kick with. She brought her heel down hard against his shin; he just grinned at her. The more she kicked, the fiercer she struggled, the wider his grin.

He let her get the fury out of her system and then, when she was trembling and spent, his mouth came down to repeat the torrid assault on lips submissive to his will, forcing her head back and making her spine arch to such a degree that she would have fallen over if he hadn't been holding her.

It would have been so easy — desirable, even — to let the burning impact of his lips defeat her and give in. But she must tell him that she was a virgin. It took all her effort and every scrap of her concentration to drag her mouth from the silencing persuasive insistence of his and gasp, "You mustn't do this, Noel. If you do you'll regret it because I'm —"

"Unwilling? That's a debatable point. But in any case I'm taking you whether you're unwilling or not, and I won't regret a thing. You've been asking for this for weeks. Taunting, drawing back. Full marks, my little temptress, for knowing what turns a man on and makes him keener. I thought it was all new to you, that I'd awakened emotions in you that you had been unaware of, that you didn't know your own power. I thought you were in conflict with your conscience when you backed away. I didn't know you were playing a very clever, if dangerous, game. Something's just occurred to me. You demanded money for silence from Jamie before you met me." Laughing down at her in angry contempt, he said, "My poor little pet, you didn't know you were going to hook a bigger fish or you would never have tried to blackmail Jamie. I'm afraid, because of that, that your worth has gone down. I won't pay the price of a wedding ring for you now. I'm not like Jamie. No mercenary little baggage is going to take me in, buy you won't go away empty-handed. I'll not be unappreciative."

"Don't, Noel. Please don't talk like this. You're speaking in anger. You don't know what you're saying."

"Don't I? You've played with my feelings, tried to make a fool of me. You *have* made a fool of me. Don't quibble now, it's pay-up time."

"I'm not quibbling. I don't know the answer to this yet, but I know I've brought a lot of it on myself. I should have taken the necessary steps to get my freedom when Jamie left me. I should have been honest with you from the beginning. I can see your side of it. Will you believe that I can't let you do this for your sake, not mine? If you do, if you go through with this, you will never forgive your—" His mouth brushed across the fast-beating pulse in her throat, changing her voice to a whisper. His fingers

182

were doing sensuous things to her body, stroking along her collarbone, discovering all the fragile little hollows, slowly exploring the curve of her breast, finding a way under the delicate peach satin of her bra. She couldn't concentrate on what she was trying to say. "You'll hate yourself if . . . when . . ." she amended, recognizing the futility, yet instinctively backing away, hampered by the length of her dress, finding each foothold with increasing difficulty. Her heel caught, the bed came up against the backs of her legs and the next moment her head was touching the softness of the quilt.

The bed gave as he added his weight to it. There was a ripping sound and then she was no longer hampered by her dress. It lay on the carpet where he had flung it, to reproach her eyes. Somehow or other he had divested himself of his robe and her of her bra, and for the first time ever her unclothed breasts molded themselves to the muscular strength of a man's naked chest.

Just for a moment she caught the look in his eyes, a bitter mingling of anger and hostility because of the deception he'd discovered in her, and self-disgust because he still wanted her. The tormented pain of his desire made his breath ragged, as if every gasp was torn tortuously from his lungs.

"You might as well give in," he said thickly. "There's no escape for you now. Your devious little mind can't come up with anything to get you out of this."

His mouth came down on hers in an explosive mixture of anger and passion, demanding a response that she refused to give, even though the effort of holding aloof made her jaw ache at being held in such a fierce clamp.

A grotesque apology for a laugh escaped his throat. "Like that, is it? Perhaps the challenge makes it all the more exciting. By the time I've finished with you, you'll be like a liquid flame in my arms. You'll have a taste of what it's like to be consumed by a driving hunger that leaves you half crazed. You won't want to hold me off; you'll beg for it."

His mouth plundered hers again. It was hard and punishing and it bruised and humiliated not just her lips, but her whole being. And yet she knew that she had brought it upon herself. It was true what Noel had said. He had revered her. The change had come about during their stay with Aunt Leonora at Kittiwake Bay. The difference in him had been little short of miraculous. He'd shrugged off his world-weary, hardened and cynical being and all the complications that went with the type of life he led and had emerged a much nicer person. She had no way of knowing whether it was the relaxing atmosphere of the place or Aunt Leonora's soothing influence, but he had shown a marked softening toward her. Even the anger she had anticipated when she refused to accept the gift of the diamond bracelet from him hadn't materialized. He had been stiff and taken aback, and he hadn't properly understood, but he hadn't lost his temper with her and she had thought perhaps it might even have worked as a point in her favor.

Right from the beginning she had been fighting his deep-rooted conviction that all women were out to take him for as much as they could get — one of the penalties he had to pay for being rich and influential. She felt sorry for him. It couldn't make for happiness to go through life with such a jaded and suspicious outlook. All women weren't like that. He had been unlucky in attracting too many of that type. She wasn't mercenary. It wouldn't have mattered to her if he didn't have a cent to his name. She had never craved for high living. Furs and jewels left her unimpressed; as far as she was concerned, a warm and loving man was worth any number of cold diamonds. All she had ever wanted was Noel's love, and she would swear that she had been almost on the brink of receiving it. Now, because she hadn't been honest with him from the start, she had destroyed her chances of ever getting that most precious of all gifts.

The sob that rose to her throat was not caused by the cruel abrasions of his hands on her body going through the motions of lovemaking without love or tenderness. That pain she could endure. She was sobbing for the way it should have been, a cherishing of kisses, caresses, shivering flesh and awe in her heart at the beauty of it.

"Don't, Noel, don't," she pleaded, finding it unbearable mental torture.

"Yes, Lorraine, yes!" he said. She could tell that the smoldering anger in him had risen above his passion; its evil was eating into his mind. "You're an exquisite little actress. Anyone would think it was your first time."

His face twisted in anguish and she knew that it bothered him to think that it wasn't. He couldn't bear the thought that someone else had known her body before him. It was an erosive and unremitting torment grinding away at his peace of mind. It gave him no rest, no respite, and his eyes burned as though his soul was barely clinging to sanity.

"Perhaps it will be the first time at that," he sneered. "Jamie is an impatient puppy. I'll show you what it's like to be made love to by a real man."

She opened her mouth to speak, but her throat was so dry the words wouldn't come. She turned her head away in misery, recoiling at the bitterness of his mockery.

"I know," he gritted, "it's not your fault. As you correctly pointed out, you had a life before we met. You're not a teen-ager."

At last she could bear no more. "I'm twenty-three. The same age my mother was when she married my father."

Why she drew that parallel she had no idea, unless her subconscious knew it would hurt him and was seeking revenge for the pain and humiliation he was causing her.

His head flicked back as though she'd taken a whip to his cheek. "I remember what you said about your parents. Your mother was worthy of being put on a pedestal. Your father was a lucky man — the first, the only one to discover the fire under the snow. I envy him. Oh, how I envy him."

You don't have to. It could be the same for you. Only her heart cried out; her brain was spinning home the message that it would serve him right to go on believing what he did. Let him suffer as he was making her suffer. But she knew she didn't mean it. She loved him too much for that.

"If I'd known from the beginning, it would have been different," he flung at her as the color drained from his face in white fury, causing her to cringe in fear. She must make him listen to her. She must tell him that if it happened now it would be the first time for her.

"Noel, I —"

"I built you up in my mind as being apart from the others," he said, drowning her out. "I wouldn't have thought you capable of keeping something so important from me. That's what makes it so hard to bear."

"What if I told you there was nothing to

bear? What if I told you I'd never been with Jamie, or with any man?" She looked directly at him, hoping the truth in her eyes would give credibility to her words.

His mouth narrowed in scathing deprecation. "I'd say that you were lying through your teeth and put it down as another of your tricks. I may have dismissed Jamie as a young pup, but his masculinity is in no doubt."

"As you know it all, I might as well save my breath," she said, pride coming to her rescue and with it a revival of her anger, because she'd tried to tell him over and over again and he wouldn't listen.

She felt like a criminal who had been convicted and sentenced without being allowed to make a plea in her own defense. There wasn't the tiniest shred of justice in his entire system.

His mouth came down on hers again, taking her by storm. It was fixed firmly in his mind that she was soiled goods, and she had thought that self-disgust had won over desire and that he'd decided not to have anything more to do with her. She had thought he was so sickened by what he thought she was that he could no longer bear to touch her.

That was not so. She could taste his sensuous hunger on her lips. She tried to keep her wits sharpened and alert, even as she knew that forces just below the surface of her skin were rising to defeat her. Perhaps she had fought too long and hard and she was both mentally and physically weakened. Instead of struggling to resist, repulsing him that way, she willed herself to a spiritual level of stony indifference. But her will was not adequate to the task, and she was soon to discover that she could not be a statue. She was a flesh-and-blood woman, and he knew how to torment every one of her body's trigger spots, awakening her tender pulse points from dormancy into delight until her brain blanked out. She knew she couldn't swim against the tide of her passions any longer, but must go along with the current of her feelings.

Her mouth was no longer merely receiving his kisses but giving them back. As he shaped her to him, her body did not resist, but molded responsively beneath his hands.

She couldn't believe it when his fingers suddenly drew away. It must have taken iron willpower to release her. He couldn't have done this to her without driving himself more than a little frantic.

Even then, she didn't think it was a calculated, vengeful maneuver, not until he spoke, his voice as cold as ice. "That's how it feels, Lorraine. That's the damnation and the torture. The disgust will follow in a little while, when you realize that you were willing to give yourself to a man who despises you, who thinks you are the lowest of the low. There are two things, above all, that I cannot abide. One is deceit; the other, blackmail, is even dirtier.

You are guilty of both."

He removed himself from the bed with the obvious intention of leaving her to contemplate her guilt and shame. Without a hearing? Perhaps it was silly of her, perhaps she should have let him go, but something in her refused to let the words go unchallenged. So she called out, arresting his step before he got to the bedroom door.

"Is that your verdict? How dare you pronounce me guilty when you won't listen to my side of it!"

He came back. There was something very menacing about his stance as he towered above her, and his clipped "Very well" was not encouraging.

"Will you please allow me the dignity of something, anything, to cover myself up?"

The nearest thing at hand was his blue silk robe, which he picked up and tossed at her, an arrogant smirk curving his mouth, which made her dig her fingernails into the palms of her hands.

"Good idea. Cover yourself up. I'll be able to concentrate better if I can't see so much of you."

Sliding into it, tying the sash tightly around her waist, she thought that while it would aid *his* concentration, wearing something as personal as his robe wasn't going to do much for hers.

Almost in despair, wishing she had waited

to explain when she was more composed, she began shakily, "I never tried to blackmail Jamie. Like you, the very thought of extorting money from someone sickens me. I never even asked Jamie to shoulder what most people considered to be his moral obligation to me."

"All right," he cut in testily, patently not believing her. "Stop belaboring the point and get on with the tale."

"What's the use, if you're not going to believe me?" she said in frustration. It all seemed so hopeless.

"You didn't make it a stipulation that I had to believe you," he sneered. "You just asked me to listen to you. Well, I'm listening. So get on with it."

She swallowed. She felt broken before she began and her voice was flat and dead, without expression or conviction. "Jamie's show-business break came on our wedding day. A big-name star fell ill and Jamie was asked to fill his place at short notice." She used much the same words she had used to explain it to Sir William, but whereas Sir William had listened kindly, Noel's countenance was hard and unyielding. She felt that she would have got more warmth by talking to a brick wall.

She battled on determinedly, telling him about the canceled honeymoon, booking into a hotel close to where Jamie was appearing, the rehearsals that tied him up for the rest of the day. "I caught the show, but for publicity reasons — you know the way of that better than I — it was thought best for me to return to the hotel by myself. Jamie stayed to have a few drinks, unwind, celebrate his success. He was an instant hit, and from that moment it all took off for him.

"To go back to that night, I got tired of sitting up for him, so I got into bed. He must have come in after I'd fallen asleep. Apparently, he was careless with a cigarette he was smoking. The first I knew of this was waking up to find that the bed was on fire. You already know about the fire and how I was badly burned."

"So Jamie was responsible. I'll admit that would give you grounds for bitterness."

"Grounds for bitterness, but not blackmail," she said doggedly.

"It doesn't come together, Lorraine. This goes back to the time that I first met Jamie. It's a pity you didn't know this or you could have altered the story to fit," he drawled sarcastically. "I signed him up on the strength of the success he had that night when he acted as stand-in. He walked into my office the next day and I knew I was buying myself a load of trouble. Just by looking at him I could tell he wouldn't be able to handle the adoration that was in store for him. I would have done him a favor if I'd shown him the door, but it went against human nature not to want a share in such a hot property. There he was — brash, blond, with his beauty unmarked. It struck me as being unusual at the time. Most male faces pick up the odd scar, relic of a schoolboy skirmish or a football tackle. The point I'm getting at is this: You say that Jamie's cigarette started the fire in which you were so terribly burned. Yet the next day he came into my office, with not as much as one single hair on his head singed. How do you account for that?"

She knew what Noel was driving at. He was asking how Jamie could have escaped unhurt from a fire that he had started. A fair question. But just for a moment she left it hanging to dwell on the thought that, while she lay so desperately ill in the hospital, Jamie's only concern had been his career.

She put her hurt aside to say, "We won't ever know the exact details of that night. I don't even know that the fire was started by a lighted cigarette. That was the finding of the forensic experts, and I'll just have to take their word for it. Jamie said he remembered coming into the room and lighting up, but he wasn't clear about much else. I woke up in a panic to find the bed on fire. My first thought was to get out of the room, which I did. I didn't know whether Jamie had come back or not. I wondered if I just might have left him in bed. So I yelled 'Fire!' at the top of my voice to alert the other hotel guests and went back into the room to make sure. I tried to beat out the flames, not knowing that Jamie wasn't there."

For the briefest moment she thought she caught a ghost-look of tenderness in his expression that wanted to comfort away the pain that remembering brought and cushion her from further hurt; but just as quickly it was gone, and, if anything, his features were more hardened against her after his momentary weakness.

"If Jamie wasn't in the bed, where was he?"

"In the bathroom," she said stiffly. "That's it. There's nothing more to tell."

"I think there is. You haven't explained how Jamie got out of the bathroom."

"He walked out," she said, flaring up in retaliation at the disbelief and sarcasm in his tone. "Don't assume that everyone's as rich as you are and can afford to stay in the class of hotel where every room has its own private bathroom. This was before Jamie's career took off, remember, and I was only just beginning to make a name for myself as a beauty consultant. All we could afford was a grotty third-rate hotel with one bathroom to each floor, and the one on our floor was way down the corridor, almost at the other end of the building. And don't ask me how Jamie managed to stumble there in his drunken condition, because I don't know." Jamie's drunkenness had been blamed for the fire at the time, but she hadn't meant to tell Noel that. He'd goaded her into it. "I was being rushed to the hospital, and I've got to rely on what other people told me." All the color drained from her face as she lived the horror of it again. She crossed her arms over her chest, as if it were possible to hold in the pain. "I'm sorry," she apologized. "I thought I could talk about it without getting emotional. I was like this the night you took me to the Cabana. It was seeing Sir William again for the first time since I'd stopped going back to the hospital for treatment. I broke up talking to him about it, but I thought that I'd got it out of my system and I wouldn't be upset again. I'm sorry."

Why, oh why had she had to bring Sir William's name into it? If he'd felt the tiniest sliver of sympathy for her, mention of that name buried it under an avalanche of scorn.

"I ought to have known that I'd be wrong about that, too. You went outside with him, I don't know where, but it had all the signs of a back-seat-of-the-car job. You returned after an indecently long time with your hair messed up and your lipstick smudged, but, of course, it's my suspicious mind that is at fault, because it was all perfectly innocent and aboveboard."

"Stop being so sarcastic. It *was* innocent. I was distressed and Sir William was comforting me."

"And I know how."

His fingers clamped to her jaw, jerking it so cruelly back that she thought her neck would snap. And then his mouth was on hers, a demanding assault that ground her lips against her teeth, forcing her head down on the bed.

As his weight came crashing beside her she was seized by a sick sensation of black anguish. She felt as though she were dissolving in misery and fear as she tried to combat the dark forces of his desire for her. Driven by jealousy and bitterness, he couldn't keep his hands off her. It was a mockery of making love. Sheer hatred would have been a better name for it.

She fought in cold desperation, twisting her body to evade the searching hands roughly pushing aside the material of her borrowed robe, only to be brought back and controlled by greater force.

"Can you honestly say that Sir William has never known your body?" he said, his splayed hands stroking down her back.

She was frantically trying to stem the reaction that was flowing up inside her at his touch. She was angry with herself for responding every time, even to his abuse, and she felt a desperate need to hit back, hating him for bringing her down to this low level of degradation.

"No, I don't deny it," she said wildly. She didn't add that she was under anaesthetic at the time that Sir William's hands were exploring her body, the purpose being to take the skin to graft onto her hands, and that he had never touched her in the way Noel meant, but only in a professional capacity.

Angry color swept up to his hairline. "You slut! You're anybody's, aren't you? You're not particular who has you!"

She couldn't resist one more dig, even though she knew that she had already gone too far. "I can't be particular," she flung at him. "Otherwise I wouldn't be here with you."

He was incensed beyond speech, but his eyes more than made up for that. They bored into her, twin missiles of malevolence and acrimony. Her heart began to hammer rapidly and the blood came singing to her ears.

"What are you going to do?" she asked in terror.

"Nothing!" he managed at length. "If I murdered you I'd be punished just as if I'd rid the world of a decent woman."

Chapter Ten

After Noel stormed out of the bedroom, rocking the door on its hinges as he slammed it shut, several minutes ticked by before she felt composed enough to check the time. It was three-thirty a.m. Obviously her wish was to go home. But how could she get there without asking Noel for his help, either to drive her or phone for a taxi for her? She looked at her ruined dress, which was all she had to wear, and lay back to sob out her humiliation and frustration.

Noel's cruelty would have been easier to bear if she had never seen his kinder side during their stay with Aunt Leonora, a side of him which had lasted right up to the time he went to America. His reason for going was to straighten Jamie out, and, like a fool, she hadn't wanted to make things worse for him by telling Noel of their involvement. If only she hadn't considered Jamie. He had never considered her. If only she'd stuck to her guns and confessed before he went. But she hadn't; she had kept silent about her marriage, and so Jamie had got in first, spinning all those lies about her trying to blackmail him. Jamie had done this to get out of a tight corner and not with the deliberate intention of hurting her. He was unaware that she even knew Noel, let alone that she was on friendly terms with him. She could see how it must have happened. She knew what it was like to be on the receiving end of Noel's anger, and Jamie had grabbed at the first thing he could think of to justify himself. A man under pressure of blackmail can be excused for going off the rails. Oh! She crumpled her hand bitterly against her mouth, trying to stem the fresh tide of despair sweeping over her. It was all so futile.

She woke suddenly, surprised to realize that she had slept. Her eyes felt hollow and unrefreshed; her head was aching from the knots of tension in her neck.

It was the intensity of Noel's gaze which had awakened her. He was fully dressed, exuding the faint smell of aftershave, and he loomed over her, his face grim and forbidding.

What was he making of her pallor, the dark shadows she knew would be under her eyes, her eyes themselves, lackluster and fearful? In his mind, did these things point to her guilt?

"Good morning," she said weakly.

"That remains to be seen. I've phoned Jamie and told him to get over here. I'm sure you won't object to a confrontation with your estranged husband?"

"I've nothing to be afraid of," she said with more confidence than she felt, before his statement got through to her. "Do you mean that you've ordered Jamie home from Las Vegas?"

"He doesn't have quite that far to travel. Didn't I tell you? I brought him back with me. He was all washed up over there. About the only thing he wasn't into was drugs. Even so, in the short time he was there he left a trail of havoc in his wake. I was lucky to get him out of the country without charges being brought against him. If you'd deliberately set out to wreck him, you couldn't have done a better job."

"He really convinced you that his phony blackmail story was on the level! You think I'm lying, not Jamie, don't you?"

"Let's put it this way. When I told Jamie to get around here because I had his wife in my apartment, he was delighted. Hardly the reaction of a man with his back against the wall. He assumed I'd set up the meeting to extricate him from your clutches, that I'd contacted you to sort out your nasty bit of blackmailing mischief. You don't look very surprised."

"No." She sighed. "I've had bitter experience of Jamie's dealings. I'm not surprised."

She had always had a nervous fear of meeting Jamie again. Apart from that one time at the club, she hadn't seen him since the day he ran from her hospital bed saying he couldn't bear to look at her mutilated hands and her terribly hurt face. She had dreaded running into him again in case it brought the old pain back. Now she dreaded it for the new grief it would bring her.

Jamie obviously intended to keep up this monstrous accusation he had made against her. Did he think he could bluff his way out? Was that his reasoning? Could he possibly have anything to back up the things he'd said?

She had truth on her side, but on his side Jamie had a lying tongue that was sometimes more plausible than the truth. He was a survivor without scruples. He would just as soon destroy her as look at her to save himself.

"How am I supposed to receive Jamie?" she inquired, lifting her chin and striving for dignity. "In your dressing gown? My dress won't hold together."

"That's been taken care of. I phoned Judith Brown, my secretary, and asked her to do some shopping for me. She's going to pick up a selection of dresses for you to choose from. With luck she should get here before Jamie."

"That's charming! She'll know I've spent the night here. What will she think?"

He shrugged. "I don't really care."

"You might not, but I do. I care about my good name."

"What good name?" he jeered.

She was still grasping around in her mind for an answer to that as he said, "I'll leave you now. By the time you've taken a shower and generally freshened up, your clothes ought to have arrived. The bathroom's through —"

"Thank you. I know where the bathroom is," she said through clenched teeth.

She returned, feeling slightly better after her shower, to find four dresses, a most worthy selection to choose from, laid out on the bed, proof of Miss Brown's arrival. Feeling the embarrassment of her situation, blushing at what Noel's secretary must be thinking, she hoped she would depart as quietly as she had come and that she wouldn't have to face her. Sighing, she put that thought from her to make her choice.

A peep at the labels told her they were her size. An accurate guess, or had Noel played detective and found the size from the label on her torn dress?

The keynote, as it so often is with expensive clothes, was elegance and simplicity. A classic cream dress embroidered with sprays of self-colored flowers was next to a chic little number in French blue. A water-ice lemon dress was cool-looking and morning fresh. A feminine swirl of soft-hued pleats caught her eye for a moment before it moved on to a starkly plain aquamarine dress with an abstract pattern. As her finger stroked over it debatingly it gained an amazing fluidity, bringing the pattern to life, and there, swimming across the sea-green material, were hundreds of tiny fish.

This one was irresistible. She dared not spare the time to preen before the mirror; Jamie could be here any minute. She noticed briefly as she combed her golden hair that the blue-green color brought out the green in her eyes.

With her hair flowing down her back, she looked like a mermaid. It might be appropriate for the dress, but it would hardly be prudent to look like a Lorelei type who attracted unsuspecting men to their doom, so she wound it expertly around her fingers into a Grecian knot. She delved into her handbag for a lipstick to run lightly across her lips. She looked good and she was glad of it. She needed all the confidence she could get.

Noel was staring broodingly out the window. He turned as she came into the room, his eyes paying her the compliment his lips withheld. They traveled slowly downward from the pale crown of her hair and then all the way up again to rest on her face.

She felt her pulses quicken at the way he looked at her, and she hated herself for not being indifferent to him, just as she knew that he was hating himself for not being indifferent to her. His silent homage had hungry depths. They tore each other apart, yet the desire burned as fiercely as ever.

An ill-founded flicker of sympathy ran through her at his hurt. He had set her up too high, and he couldn't lower his ideals. She suffered his pain with him. She must fight Jamie, no matter what he threw at her. She must see that the truth prevailed, for Noel's sake, because it was destroying him to think this badly of her.

But when he spoke, sounding so cold and

civilized, she wondered if her sympathy was not misplaced. "My secretary is in the kitchen, making herself useful with the coffeepot."

"What have you told her?"

"The basic facts. That Jamie's wife is here and that Jamie is coming around. I warned her it might get unpleasant."

"I could have made the coffee. It wasn't fair of you to involve her."

"Me involve her? Surely you did that when you harassed her into giving you Jamie's address."

"I made one call. That's not harassing anyone. And she didn't give me his address."

"I'd stay and argue the point, but I think I hear Jamie now. Yes, that will be him."

As Noel went to open the door, her fingers moved protectively to the palpitating pulse in her throat. She wondered how a pulse could function there at all, because her neck felt like a column of ice; as Jamie came into the room it was as though she were swallowing icicles.

That one time she saw Jamie at Noel's club, she had been sitting too far back to see him properly. Perhaps she had painted that youthful face from memory, or perhaps clever stage makeup had concealed the ravages of time; but viewed across the room, Jamie looked every day of his age and even several years more. The rich living he had craved was beginning to tell. His weak, handsome face had acquired a slight puffiness. It was barely discernible now, but if he kept up his present lifestyle it would not be long before he lost his sweet, angelic look of good, wholesome living.

Noel had said that he'd warned Jamie that she would be here, but as she came within his range of vision she could have sworn that he was surprised — no, the word surprise was too bland, too much of an understatement. He seemed horrified to see her. As his reaction registered on her brain, distress and reciprocal horror raged through her to hold still every functioning thought in her mind. A shroud of numbness came down to envelop her. She struggled, using every particle of mental energy she was able to summon up, to make any kind of sense of the dismay sagging Jamie's mouth and the petrified disbelief glazing his eyes.

Dear and merciful God, no! Because the look on Jamie's face was almost, but not quite, the twin of the one she'd seen when he visited her in the hospital. He hadn't been able to bear looking at the mutilations she had suffered in the fire and had backed away from her in repugnance.

For one icily sick moment she was back in those black days, swathed in the grievous pain of it all to such an extent that she wondered if the intervening healing years had really happened or if she had dreamed them. A manifestation conjured up by her tortured mind of what she hoped one day would come to be.

She looked down at her hands, cringing in

fear of what she might see, but they were smooth and healed. As she touched one over the other for reassurance, a wondrous sense of relief filled her throat and made her feel almost light-headed. Yet that same relief gave her an even greater desire to know what it was all about and, at the same time, somehow made it possible for her to reason more clearly. Dismay had been keener than horror on Jamie's face. He had walked into this room conditioned to see his wife. Well, she was Jamie's wife, wasn't she? Yet he had been surprised to see her!

As her eyes flashed at him, puzzled and angrily demanding an explanation, Jamie's mouth was already in the process of forming a reply. It shaped to say her name in silence and then the words exploded from him in ragged agony. "Lorraine! I didn't expect to see you . . ."

He stopped speaking with an abruptness that made the ensuing silence all the more profound and his hands lifted in a gesture that expressed so much but told so little. Jamie was a performer, and now that he had got over the initial shock of seeing her he was able to draw heavily on his professional expertise to cover up.

It was Noel who pounced on him, surveying him through shrewd eyes. "You didn't expect to see Lorraine?" he challenged. "How come? I told you that I had your wife here."

His wife, not me, Lorraine thought. The speculation spun dizzily in her head. She had no idea where it came from, or what sense could be made of it.

"My — ?" began Jamie. The question-held pause was so slight as to be almost indiscernible; the feeling of query was just as instantly turned into the proudest of declarations. "My wife," he said with astounding boldness and assurance. "My *beautiful* wife. That's what took me by surprise, what I meant. I didn't expect to see Lorraine looking so devastatingly lovely. Lorraine," he said, turning his attention from Noel to her. "You are so beautiful."

Whatever else was false about the situation, it was not that. The words came out sincerely, voicing his true thoughts, and gave credibility to his reaction. She was being unduly suspicious, looking for something that wasn't there. He hadn't been surprised to see her; he was surprised to see her as she was now, not ugly and gruesome anymore.

He came over to where she was sitting and knelt before her to take her hands in his. Last time they met he couldn't bear to look at her; now he couldn't seem to take his eyes off her. She could feel the lust washing over her.

"How could I have let you go?" he moaned. "I must have been out of my mind."

His nerve was incredible. She dragged her hands away, cringing in revulsion at his touch just as he had cringed from her in revulsion when she had been hurt and had needed him so desperately. Jamie was down now, and it was just possible that he needed her; but she felt nothing for him. The agony he had put her through had killed every bit of love and tender feeling she must once have had for him.

Jamie was still speaking, attempting to take her hands back and looking at her in the old remembered way with the melting, little-boy appeal which she had been unable to resist. It did nothing for her now; even though she was trapped in this hideous situation, she felt gloriously free on that point.

"Don't be angry with me," he implored. "I know I shouldn't have walked out on you, but don't you see, it was because I loved you so much that I couldn't stand to see you so hurt."

"No, Jamie," she said resolutely. "If you'd loved me you would have stayed and given me the support I needed."

"I wasn't strong enough, Lorraine. You know what I'm like. I can't help how I'm made. I need to have beauty around me. I couldn't know you'd get your looks back. I've made such a mess of everything. But — we can put it all behind us, darling. Make a fresh start. Things will work out, you'll see."

Before she could reply, Noel said in jealous fury, "It seems that you have been granted a full pardon, Lorraine."

"Pardon?" she said, grappling for understanding. Ridiculous as it might seem, with all the other crowding of emotions she had forgotten the blackmail charge that Jamie had made against her. Remembering, she said wearily, "I haven't done anything wrong."

"No?" Noel said, and although she looked deep into his eyes his expression was unreadable.

He then took Jamie roughly by the arm, hauled him to his feet and tossed him into a chair. "Now listen to me, you sniveling little creep. It's time you realized that you can't drop people when the going's tough and then come back and expect to find everything the same. You had your chance with Lorraine and passed it up."

"What's it to you whether or not Lorraine and I make it up?" Jamie said sulkily.

"That's my business," Noel replied curtly. "But I'll tell you one thing. You needn't be worried about being blackmailed anymore. I'll see to it that all that nonsense is dropped."

"How can I drop something I've never done in the first place?" Lorraine broke in desperately. "Tell him, Jamie, that I've never on any occasion been in contact with you since my time in the hospital. And for the sake of my sanity, I implore you, please tell *me* what it's all about."

But Jamie remained hunched and silent in his chair, and, although Noel was sending him searching, angry looks that might indicate a softening in his attitude toward her, it was apparent that he still thought Jamie's story contained an essential element of truth.

It was like a nightmare she could see no way

out of. She couldn't get through to anyone, and suddenly it was all too much for her. She clenched her fingers and began to cry. Hysteria, frustration — all these things went into the desperate sounds coming from her throat.

Noel's long body ejected itself from his chair. He reached forward to grasp hold of her arms, and he shook her until her teeth chattered. She knew he was doing it to calm her down.

"Stop it. This isn't doing any good at all," he condemned sternly.

"Nothing does any good," she said, choking on a sob. "I can't make anyone believe me. I'm going to divorce you, Jamie, and I don't want to see you ever again. And that goes for you, too, Noel. Goodbye. I'm getting out of here before I really break down."

"You're not going anywhere in this state. Jamie — you'll find Judith in the kitchen. Tell her to hurry up with that coffee. A shot of something in it might be a good idea for Lorraine."

"Just coffee," she said, exhausted after her lapse and realizing the futility of trying to fight against Noel's strength of mind and physical superiority.

He waited until Jamie had disappeared into the kitchen, watching to make sure that he'd closed the door behind him. His hands were still on her arms, and she knew that if she pulled away she would be brought closer. Noel couldn't have her this near and not want her, and the same went for her. His eyes could pierce her with steel-gray contempt, as indeed they were doing, and his brows could be drawn in disapproval, but, to her shame, it made no difference in the way she felt about him.

He groaned and drew her fully into his arms, his lips brushing abrasively across the hair that he had once likened to spun gold, and he avenged his anger on her in the cruel, bruising tightness of his hold. It was as though he had to punish her for the way he felt about her. Their touching bodies radiated shock waves of passion that neither could deny. The heat of their mutual desire seemed to fuse them together, and the willpower she had to pit against this was next to useless.

"I can't do without you," he said, his cutting tone tearing through her. "I know you for what you are — a scheming, deceiving little blackmailer — yet I still want you. I mean to have you, even if I have to marry you."

She was close to tears. If only she were the scheming, deceiving blackmailer he thought she was. If only her nature would allow her to accept such a bitter proposal in the hope that in time he would really see her as she was. But it was no good. She couldn't stoop to such degradation. The only marriage proposal she could accept would be one tendered with love.

"No!" she said, shaking her head vehemently. "I take it that I should be overwhelmed with gratitude that you can bring yourself to marry me in view of everything, but I'm not. Such a proposal is an insult and totally unacceptable."

"You mean you're turning me down?" he asked, stunned.

"I most certainly am."

She hadn't heard the door open, and she didn't think he had, either. But as his arms slackened to release her, she swung around to see Jamie — and a woman in a tailored suit, brown hair speckled with gray, a face with mortification at what she had obviously just seen and heard, carrying a laden tray in none too steady fingers.

"I'm most dreadfully sorry, sir," she began. "I didn't mean to intrude."

"Stop flapping, Judith," Noel grunted irritably. "It doesn't matter. Just put that blasted tray down before you drop it."

As the poor bewildered woman looked for a surface upon which to deposit it, Noel indicated a coffee table.

Jamie took the opportunity to whisper in Lorraine's ear, "I didn't realize you were the big chief's property. This puts a whole new light on the matter." His expression turned first speculative, then gleeful. "You'll marry him, of course. You could do me some good. Put in a good word. Get him to change his mind about washing his hands of me and, instead, use your influence to make him smooth things over for me. His opinion counts in a big way. Why, with his backing I could be right back there at the top."

She glared at him. "I do not intend to marry Noel Britton. I have no influence with him. And you, Jamie Gray, are impossible!" And predictable to the end. Still thinking only of himself.

She sat down. Judith Brown handed a cup of coffee to her, her eyes glancing curiously over Lorraine as she did so, almost as if she wondered who she was and where she fitted in.

But she knew who she was. Noel had told her. Yet the conviction was strong in Lorraine's mind that Noel's secretary had expected to see someone else. Judith Brown's reaction on seeing her was too close to Jamie's not to set her thoughts buzzing again. Until she realized she was doing what she had done before, grasping at straws. Seeing something she wanted to see which wasn't there.

Everything had a logical explanation. Considering Noel's close working relationship with many glamorous females, Judith Brown might well be used to walking in and finding him in a compromising situation. But Lorraine thought it might be the first time she'd overheard him proposing marriage. It would have given her an even bigger jolt to hear him being turned down. There couldn't be many girls around who would say no to such a prize catch. That's why she had looked her over so curiously.

And then, just as all hope had gone, Judith Brown dropped her sweet bombshell.

"Has Mrs. Gray left?" she inquired, so quietly, so unexpectedly.

"This is Mrs. Gray," Noel replied, nodding toward Lorraine, his eyes, his whole manner, electrically alert.

Jamie had gone as white as a sheet. The atmosphere was tense.

"You're mistaken, sir. At least," she added, a flicker of confusion crossing her features, "it's not the Mrs. Gray who came around asking for Jamie's address."

Jamie was biting his knuckles.

"Explain!" Noel commanded.

"I didn't know your secretary had ever seen Mandy. You said she'd phoned to get my address."

Judith Brown answered for herself. "So she did. She was more persistent than the other girls who rang saying they needed to get in touch with you. She bombarded me with phone calls, but the policy is not to give out addresses. So then she came around to the club. She was in such a state that, well, I broke the golden rule and told her where you were staying."

"Who is Mandy?" Lorraine asked sharply.

Jamie shrugged and admitted after a lengthy pause, "My wife."

"But *I'm* your wife."

"Not legally. I'm sorry, Lorraine, and you'll never know how much, but I was already married when we supposedly tied the knot. When Mr. Britton said he'd got my wife here, I expected to see her. I got the shock of my life

214

when I walked in and saw you. It seemed best to bluff it out. It nearly came off, too."

"You mean, you committed . . . bigamy?"

He nodded. "I suppose that's the word for it." Addressing Noel, he said, "Of course, it's Mandy who is putting the squeeze on, not Lorraine. She found out that I'd gone through a marriage ceremony with Lorraine and decided it was good for a spot of blackmail." He turned back to Lorraine. "I was only eighteen when I married her. She was four years older. It didn't work out."

"Why didn't you tell me?"

"That's obvious." His lifted eyebrows implied surprise that she should have to ask. "You wouldn't have had anything to do with me if I had."

Astounded at his audacity, she said fiercely, "Too true, I wouldn't! How could you have done this to me? How could you go through the pretense of a wedding ceremony knowing that you were already married?"

"I swear it wasn't like that. Mandy had started divorce proceedings, and I thought it had gone through. But, like a woman, she changed her mind and informed her solicitor to drop the case. You know how it is in show business. I was on the road at the time, with no permanent address. By the time the solicitor's letter caught up with me, giving me the facts, it was too late because I'd already gone through that ceremony with you. That's God's truth."

She shook her head, trying to take it in, and then accused chokingly, "It wasn't too late to tell me when you found out. It was cruel of you to let me go on believing we were married."

As her voice shuddered to a stop, Noel's steadying hand made contact with her shoulder before he charged across the room to yank Jamie out of his chair. It flashed through her mind what he intended to do, but he was in action before she could put in a word of protest. His fist smashed against Jamie's face with such violence and force that Jamie was sent spinning into the air. He crashed back down onto the coffee table, which shattered under the impact, sending crockery flying and hot coffee splashing in all directions.

"Noel — I think you've broken his nose," Lorraine gasped out, thinking how dreadful it was that something like this should happen to Jamie, who put such a price on good looks. Her thoughts were ludicrous in the face of his defection, but it felt wonderful to pity Jamie. To know that she wasn't bitter any more and that her cure was quite complete.

"If I have, it's no more than he deserves," Noel gritted out savagely. "I ought to have killed the swine for what he's put you through." He added something under his breath which Lorraine was not meant to hear.

Judith Brown was fully occupied recoiling in fascinated horror from the spectacle that Jamie presented. "He looks very bloody," she observed. "He'll be scarred for life."

"I always did say he was too beautiful for a man. He'll probably look better for it. I certainly feel better for it," Noel said unrepentantly, nursing his knuckles. "Phone someone to get him removed, Judith."

She did so at once, phoning for an ambulance, and when it arrived she volunteered to go with Jamie to the hospital.

Noel came back from seeing them off at the door. Lorraine was attempting to clear up the broken china.

"Leave it," he instructed, lifting her from her kneeling position and taking her into his arms.

They had been through a highly emotional ordeal. The trauma of months was in the shaking of her limbs and the unsteadiness of his voice as he said, "My darling, I've put you through unforgivable torture. I should have believed you. I shouldn't have behaved the way I did. I don't know how to begin to say I'm sorry."

Her fingers closed over his mouth. "Don't try. The nightmare is over. That's all that matters." She shuddered, not in fear or horror, but in intense and wonderful relief. "I'm not married to Jamie! That's almost too wonderful to believe. Ending a marriage is so sad. I should have felt hollow, somehow, even though Jamie and I never had a proper marriage in the first place. I don't even feel vindictive toward Jamie anymore. I'm far too happy. I feel rather sorry for him, because what he said is true — he can't help the way he's made. Poor Jamie. If you feel as though you can keep him under contract, I'd be quite pleased. I'd like to think he had a chance to make something of himself."

"You're incredible! I'm afraid I'm less forgiving than you. I'll think about it, but I'm making no rash promises," he said. "I'll get my solicitor to make sure that you're in the clear — a mere formality to keep on the right side of the law — and then, if you'll have me, we'll get married. My love, please say yes. Show me the same forgiveness that you've shown to Jamie. Give me the chance you would have me give him. Let me make it up to you for how badly I've treated you."

"Oh, Noel, of course, my answer is yes."

"Thank God for that, even though I don't deserve you. I've been so eaten up with jealousy that I haven't been able to see straight. I've gone through hell imagining what you were to Sir William. That night when you went outside with him at the Cabana and brought him back to our table, I could barely talk civilly to him. Last night when you told me you were married to Jamie Gray I thought I would go mad. I know now that my obsession with wanting to be the first man to know you was unreasonable. I don't mind now that I'm not the first — I just want to be the last. "

"You're tormenting yourself unnecessarily.

I've tried to tell you so many times. You will be the first, and the last. Jamie was involved in rehearsals immediately after that bogus marriage ceremony, and we hadn't slept together before then. That's the truth."

"Oh, my darling," he said, gathering her closer, "I'm the luckiest of men. The fire under the snow. Mine to discover. I'll keep it lovingly tended. I'll devote the rest of my life to doing just that. It will never burn out."

His mouth sought hers, as though sealing a pledge. It was the most heady delight to be able to indulge the tumultuous craving inside her instead of fighting to repulse it. Her lips returned his kisses with fervor and total abandon. All restrictions removed, nothing to inhibit or restrain her, her fingers flattened against the muscular hardness of his chest, dragging upward to link around his neck.

The closeness of her body stole his voice away and left him with only a husky remnant to whisper endearments in her ear, every word, every syllable accompanied by a caress.

His hands were tender, sweet torment and it was even more wildly wonderful than she had imagined it could be. As her longing flared, she strained closer still. She felt the unmistakable response of his body and knew that they were rapidly reaching a point where kisses and caresses would not be enough.

He held her away for a moment to look at her face, which glowed with golden rapture. He took it in his hands and his eyes hallowed every facet of her expression; his voice was broken and ragged as he said, "I love you. I adore you. I worship you."

"Not on a pedestal," she pleaded hoarsely. "Don't ever put me up there again."

"I won't. I can safely promise that. I won't ever allow your sweet body to be that far away — from the moment I've put a ring on your finger. Until then I'm going to have to hold you at arm's length."

"You don't have to."

A tortured groan came from his lips. "You know what you're saying, don't you?"

She nodded without shame. "I'm saying I want to take up from where we left off last night."

He groaned softly. "So do I. You only just told me in time that you are a virgin. I've a feeling that if you'd put it off any longer I would have found out for myself. As it is, I must wait, however much of a strain I find it. Heaven will bless this marriage, and I'm not going to do anything to defile it. It's important for it to be right from the very beginning, because it's going to last us a lifetime."

"I wouldn't have told you if I'd known," she said, but she was secretly pleased, because his strong views on the subject matched her own. "Noel, there's something I want to ask you, something that would please me very much."

"I'll grant any wish but one. I won't agree to

a long engagement."

"A long engagement wouldn't be a wish; it would be a curse. I'll marry you as quickly as it can be arranged."

He laughed in delight at that and said, "So what do you want, my darling?"

Not quite sure how he would take this, she said hesitantly, "In cases like mine, when the bride hasn't got a father, it's customary to ask a favorite uncle to give her away. I haven't got one of those, either. So — please don't be angry — I'd like Sir William. He's the nearest to an uncle I've got. And pretty soon, if Aunt Leonora will have him, he will be my uncle."

"I don't know whether it's because you've worded it so cleverly or because I find it difficult to refuse you anything when you're this close. You have my permission to ask Sir William. Now, why don't you phone Leonora and tell her the news? While you're about it, you can give my mother a shock, in the nicest possible sense. Call her and introduce yourself as her soon-to-be daughter-in-law."

"May I? I'd love that. What will you do?"

"I'll listen to you, gloat, look at you. If I can't have you, I can anticipate." But instead of releasing her, his hold tightened. "You wouldn't deny me a little something to keep me going, would you?"

Her response to his kiss told him, more eloquently than words, that she would deny him nothing.

We hope you have enjoyed this Large Print book. Other G.K. Hall & Co. or Chivers Press Large Print books are available at your library or directly from the publishers.

For more information about current and upcoming titles, please call or write, without obligation, to:

Publisher
G.K. Hall & Co.
295 Kennedy Memorial Drive
Waterville, ME   04901
Tel. (800) 223-1244
Tel. (800) 223-6121

OR

Chivers Press Limited
Windsor Bridge Road
Bath BA2 3AX
England
Tel. (0225) 335336

All our Large Print titles are designed for easy reading, and all our books are made to last.